JULES VERNE'S

AROUND THE WORLD IN
80 DAYS

A GRAPHIC NOVEL
BY CHRIS EVERHEART
& TOD SMITH

Graphic Revolve is published by Stone Arch Books
A Capstone Imprint
1710 Roe Crest Drive, North Mankato, Minnesota 56003
www.capstonepub.com

Cataloging-in-Publication Data is available at the Library
of Congress website.
Hardcover ISBN: 978-1-4965-0373-2
Paperback ISBN: 978-1-4965-0381-7
Ebook PDF ISBN: 978-1-4965-2319-8

Summary: In London, 1872, a man named Phileas Fogg
makes a bet with his friends that he can travel across
the entire planet in eighty days. The wager? More than
half his sizable fortune — and the exact same amount of
money that was stolen from a nearby bank a day earlier.
Fogg hastily departs in the company of Passepartout,
his personal attendant, on a journey that will take the
two men all over the wide world by way of every known
means of transportation. Little does Fogg know that a sly
detective trails his every globetrotting step.

Common Core back matter written by Dr. Katie Monnin

Maps credit: Dreamstime: Richard Thomas

Designer: Bob Lentz

Printed in the United States of America in Stevens Point,
Wisconsin.
052015   008824WZ15

TABLE OF CONTENTS

ALL ABOUT AROUND THE WORLD IN 80 DAYS

Jules Verne published *Around the World in 80 Days* in 1873. Originally written in French, the book's title was *Le tour du monde en quatre-vingts jours.* It has since been translated into nearly every language spoken on Earth and proven to be a classic all across the world.

During their approximately 80-day journey, Jean, Phileas, and Aouda take a wide variety of transportation methods, including trains, steamer ships, elephants, and a wind powered sledge (similar to a sailboat that travels over snow).

Several obstacles get in their path, but like the industrial revolution at the time of Verne's writing, nothing can stop the near-locomotive force of Phileas Fogg's conviction and creativity in problem solving. With an iron will, they barrel through blockades and sneak past a determined detective with relative ease — and occasionally high risk.

Around the World in 80 Days is a story about journeys, adventure, and the industrial age. But at its heart, the story speaks to a love of travel, people, and cultures. Perhaps that is why the book has been adapted to a wide variety of different media, including movies, plays, radio, musicals — and graphic novels like this one!

CAST OF CHARACTERS

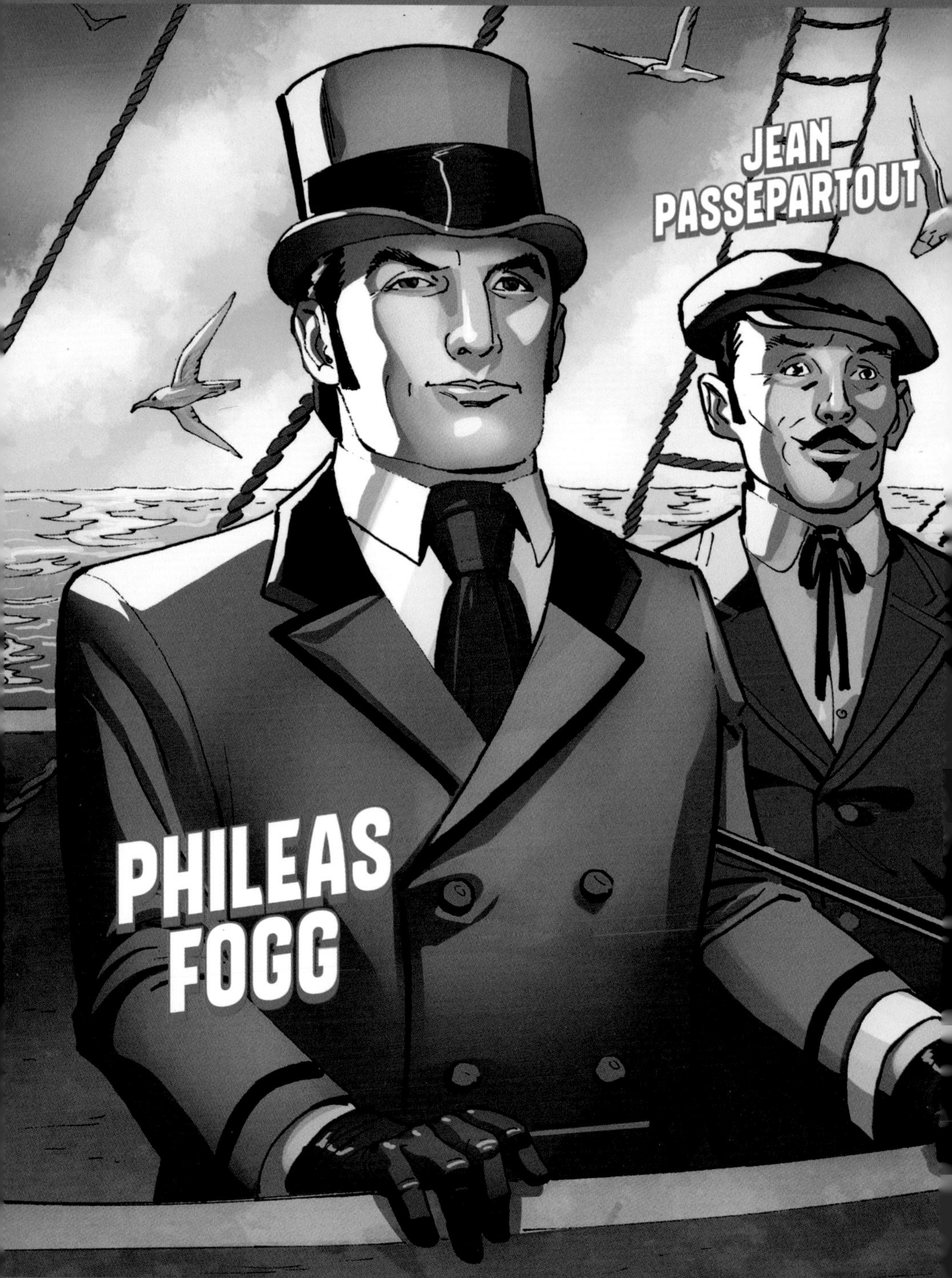
JEAN PASSEPARTOUT
PHILEAS FOGG

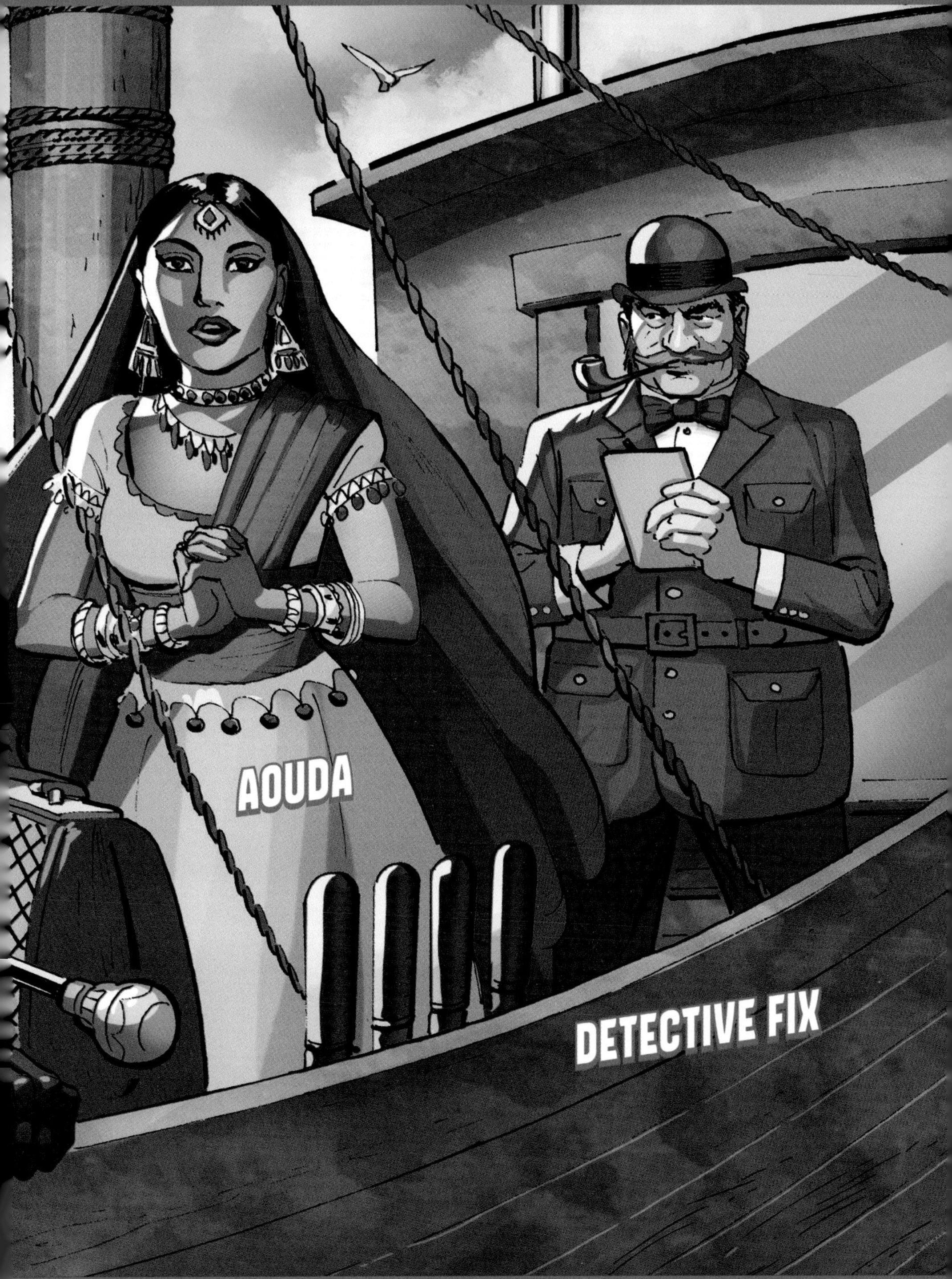
AOUDA
DETECTIVE FIX

CHAPTER 1
THE WAGER

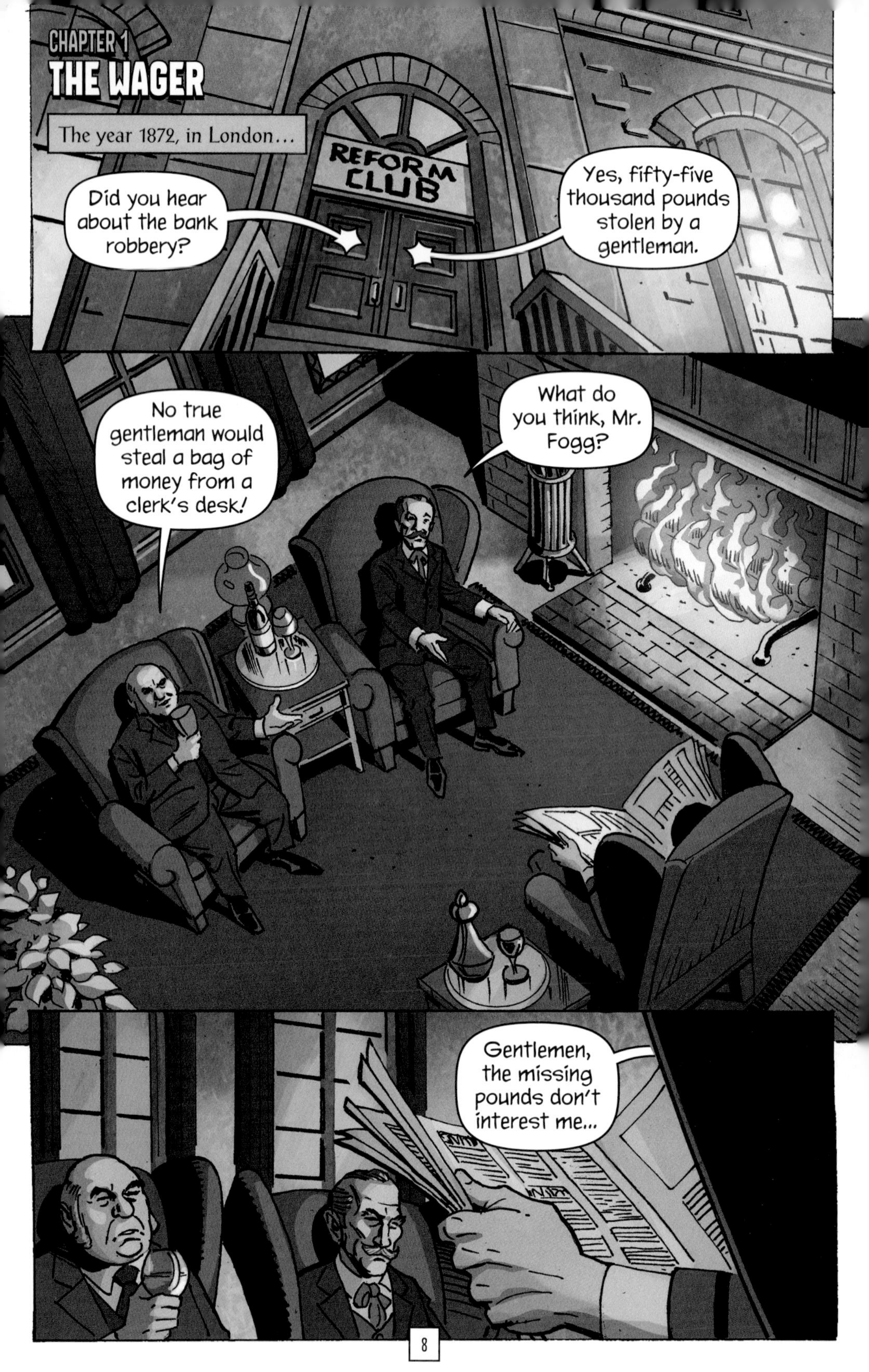

The year 1872, in London...
REFORM CLUB
Did you hear about the bank robbery?
Yes, fifty-five thousand pounds stolen by a gentleman.
No true gentleman would steal a bag of money from a clerk's desk!
What do you think, Mr. Fogg?
Gentlemen, the missing pounds don't interest me...

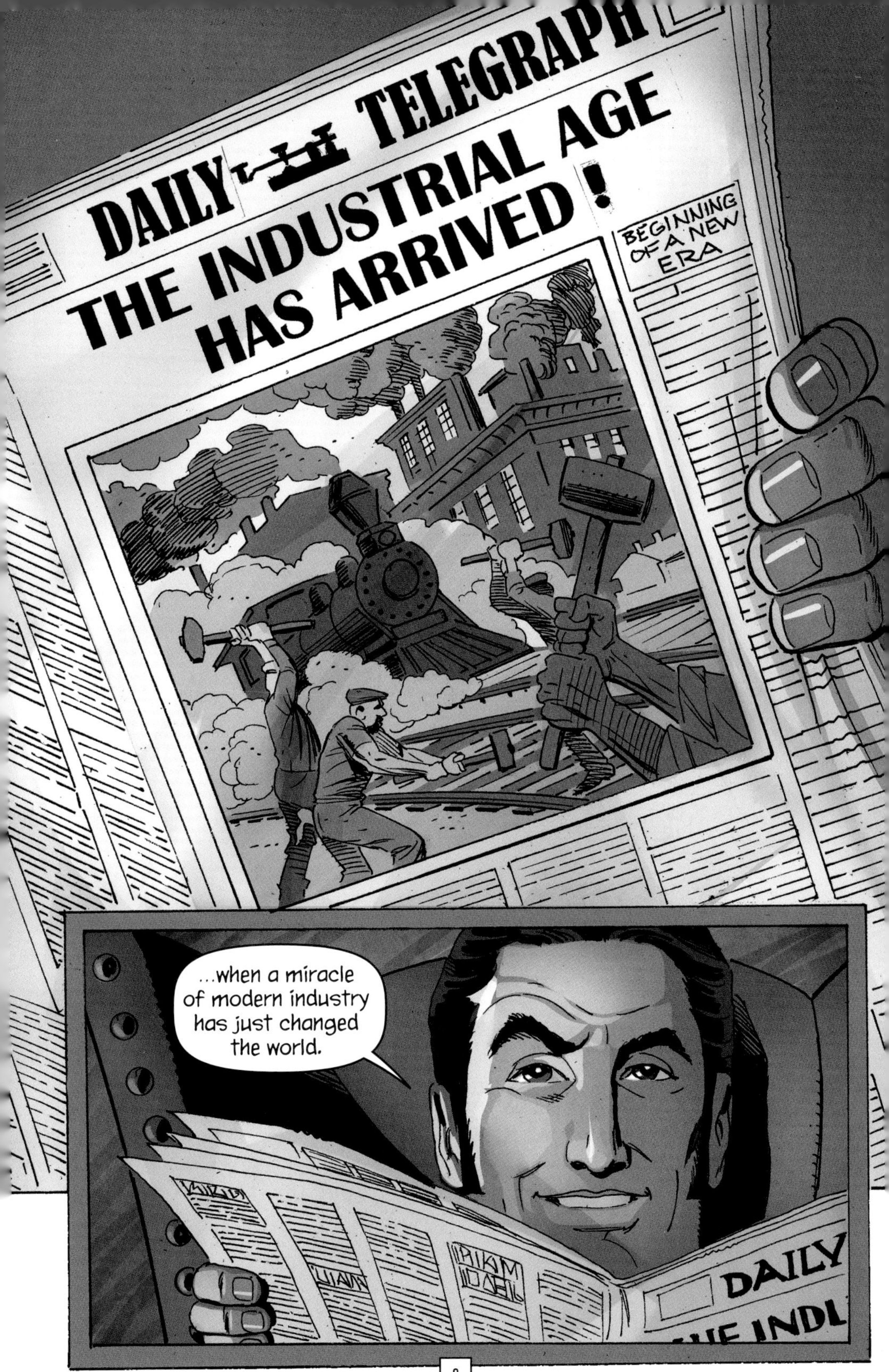
DAILY TELEGRAPH
THE INDUSTRIAL AGE HAS ARRIVED!
BEGINNING OF A NEW ERA
...when a miracle of modern industry has just changed the world.
DAILY

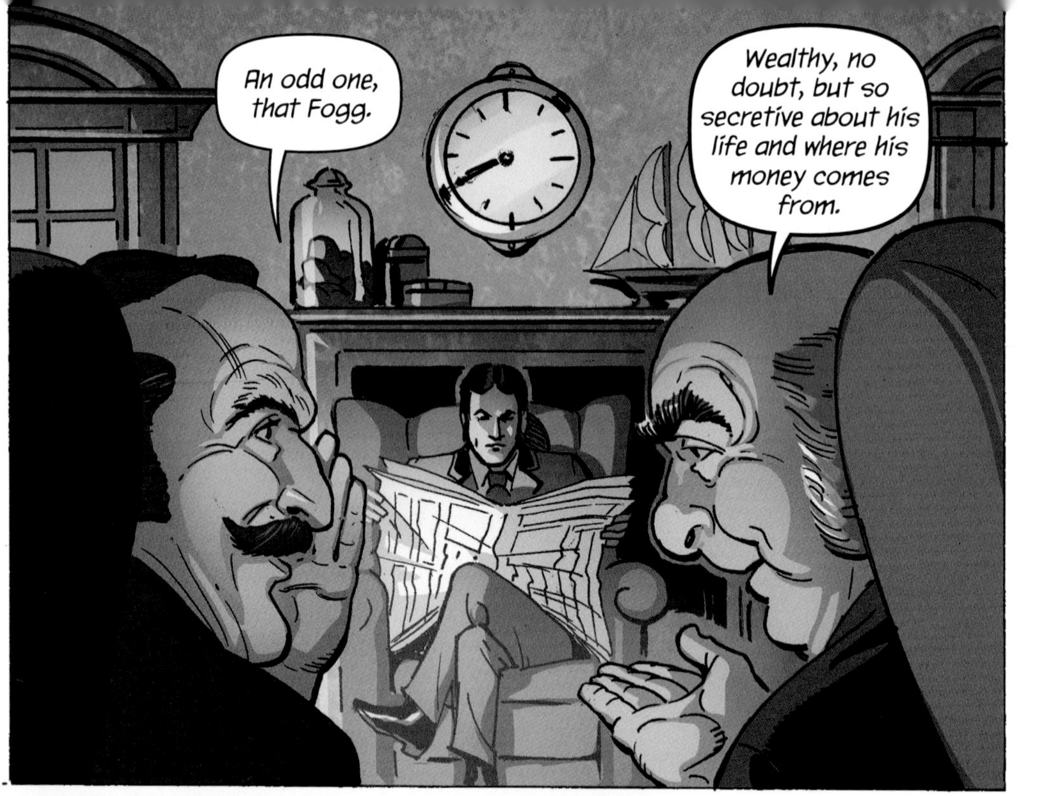
An odd one, that Fogg.
Wealthy, no doubt, but so secretive about his life and where his money comes from.

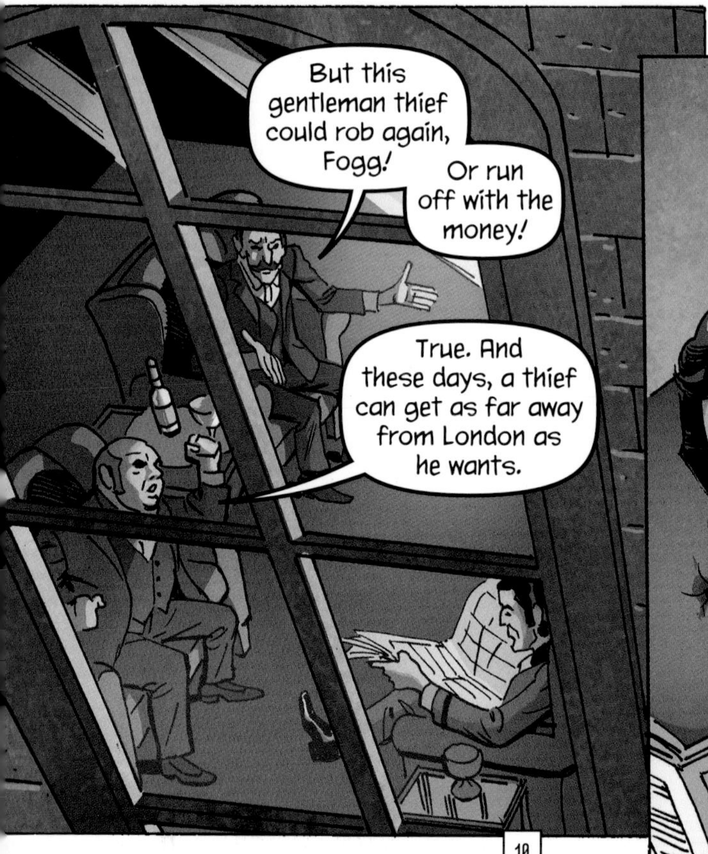
But this gentleman thief could rob again, Fogg!
Or run off with the money!
True. And these days, a thief can get as far away from London as he wants.

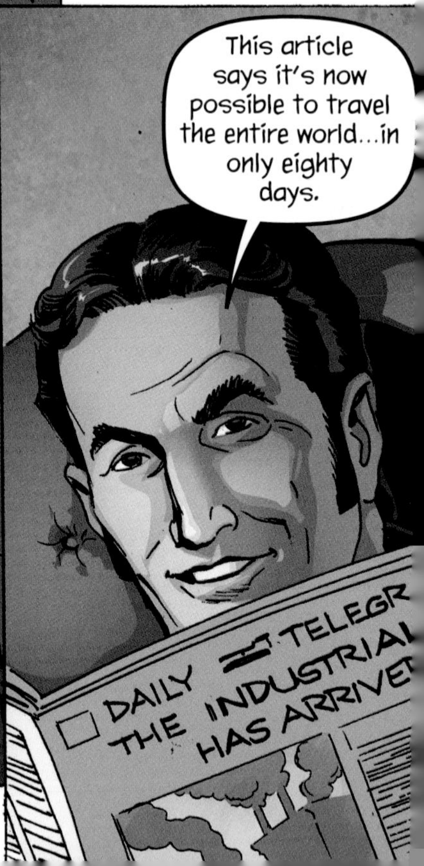
This article says it's now possible to travel the entire world...in only eighty days.
DAILY TELEGR
THE INDUSTRIAL
HAS ARRIVE

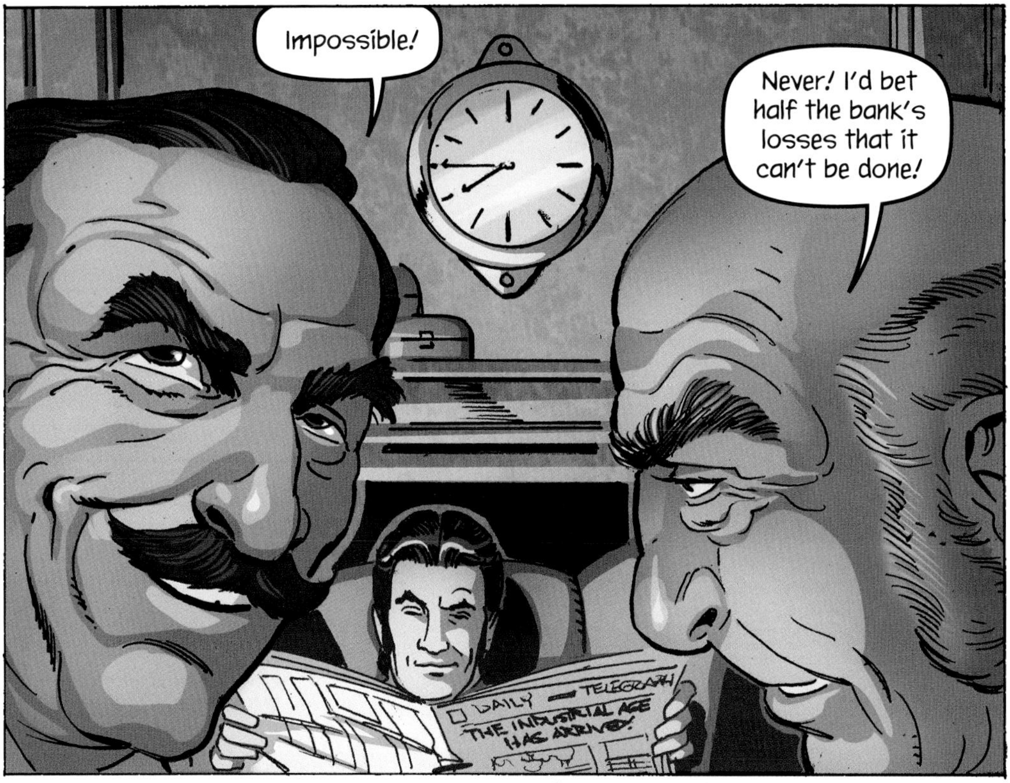
Impossible!
Never! I'd bet half the bank's losses that it can't be done!
DAILY TELEGRAPH
THE INDUSTRIAL AGE HAS ARRIVED!

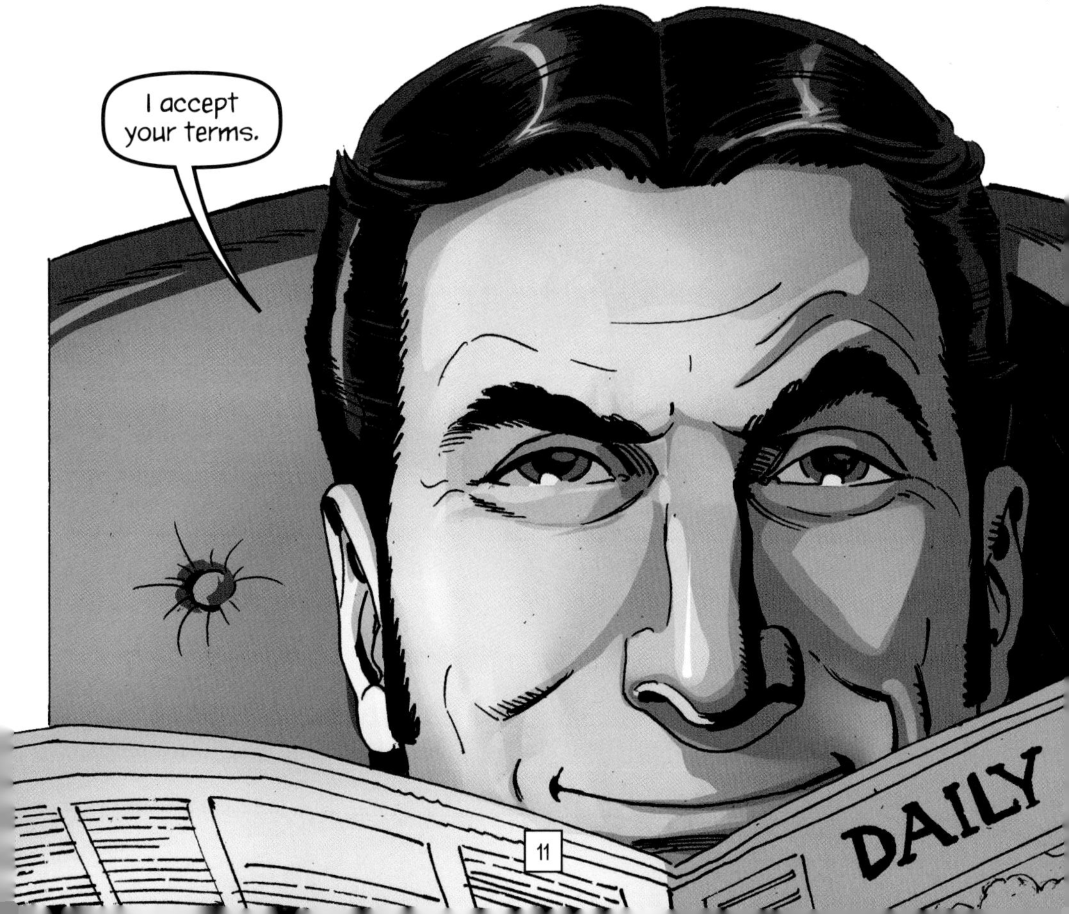
I accept your terms.
DAILY

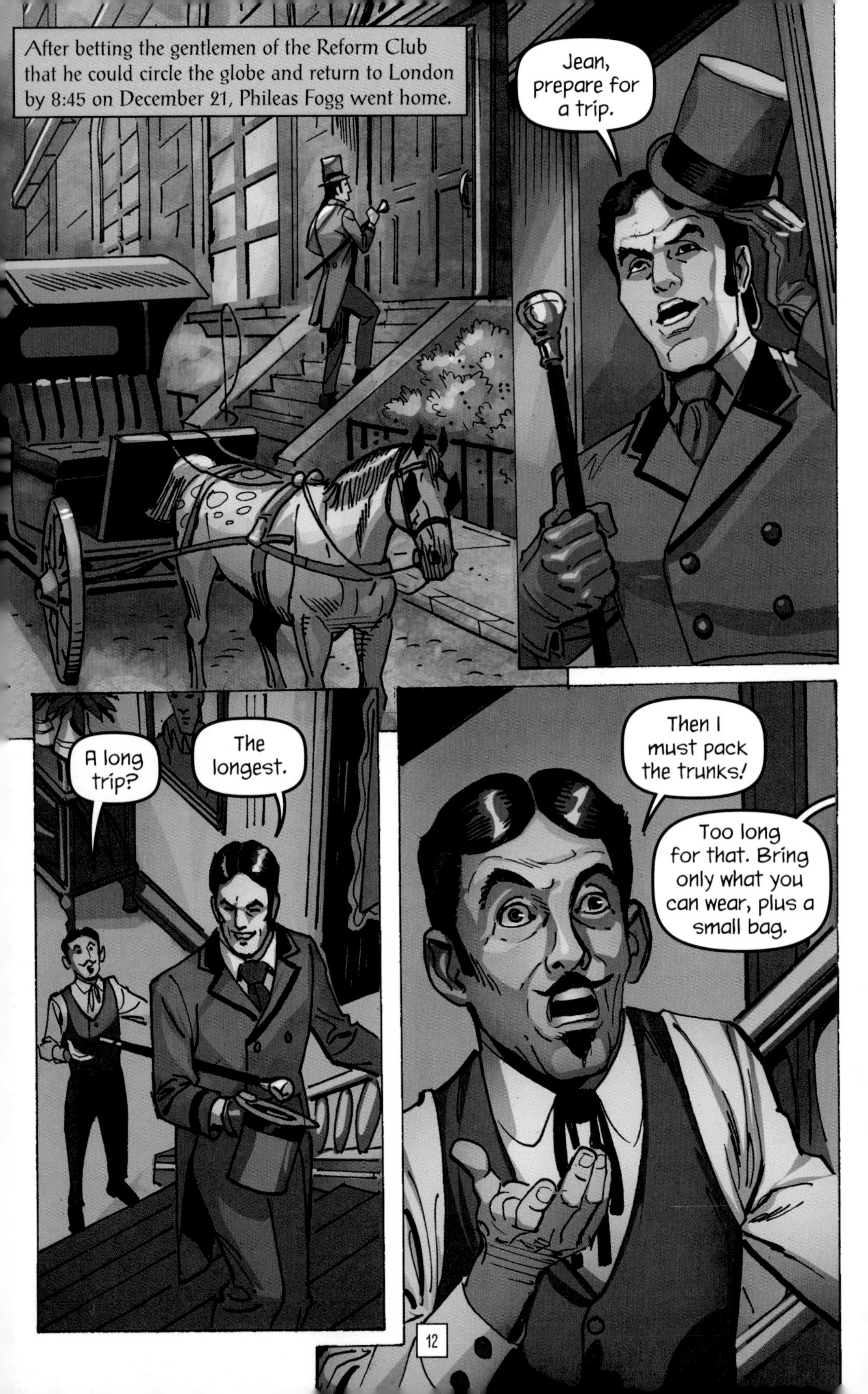
After betting the gentlemen of the Reform Club that he could circle the globe and return to London by 8:45 on December 21, Phileas Fogg went home.
Jean, prepare for a trip.
A long trip?
The longest.
Then I must pack the trunks!
Too long for that. Bring only what you can wear, plus a small bag.

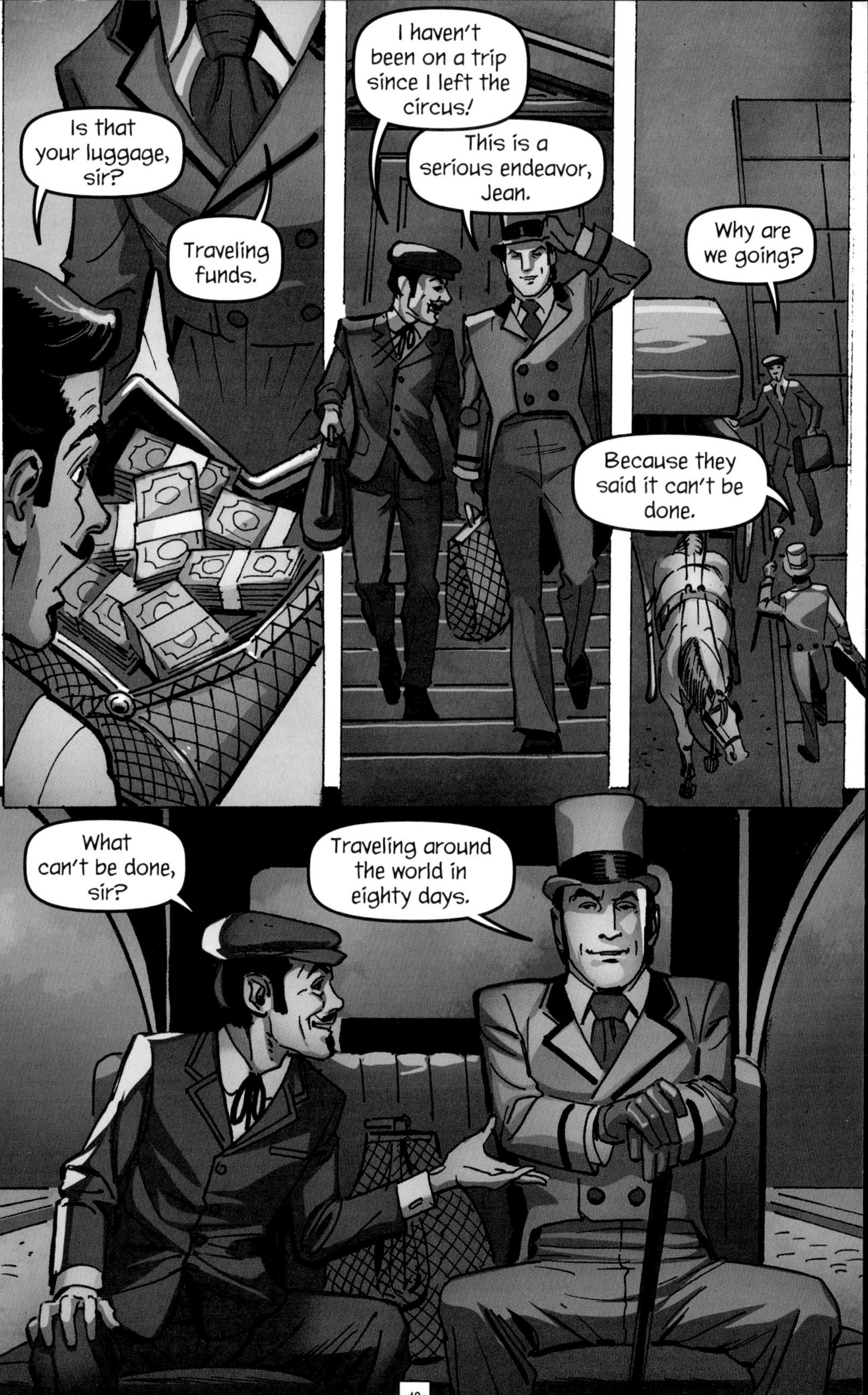
Is that your luggage, sir?
Traveling funds.
I haven't been on a trip since I left the circus!
This is a serious endeavor, Jean.
Why are we going?
Because they said it can't be done.
What can't be done, sir?
Traveling around the world in eighty days.

CHAPTER 2
THE JOURNEY

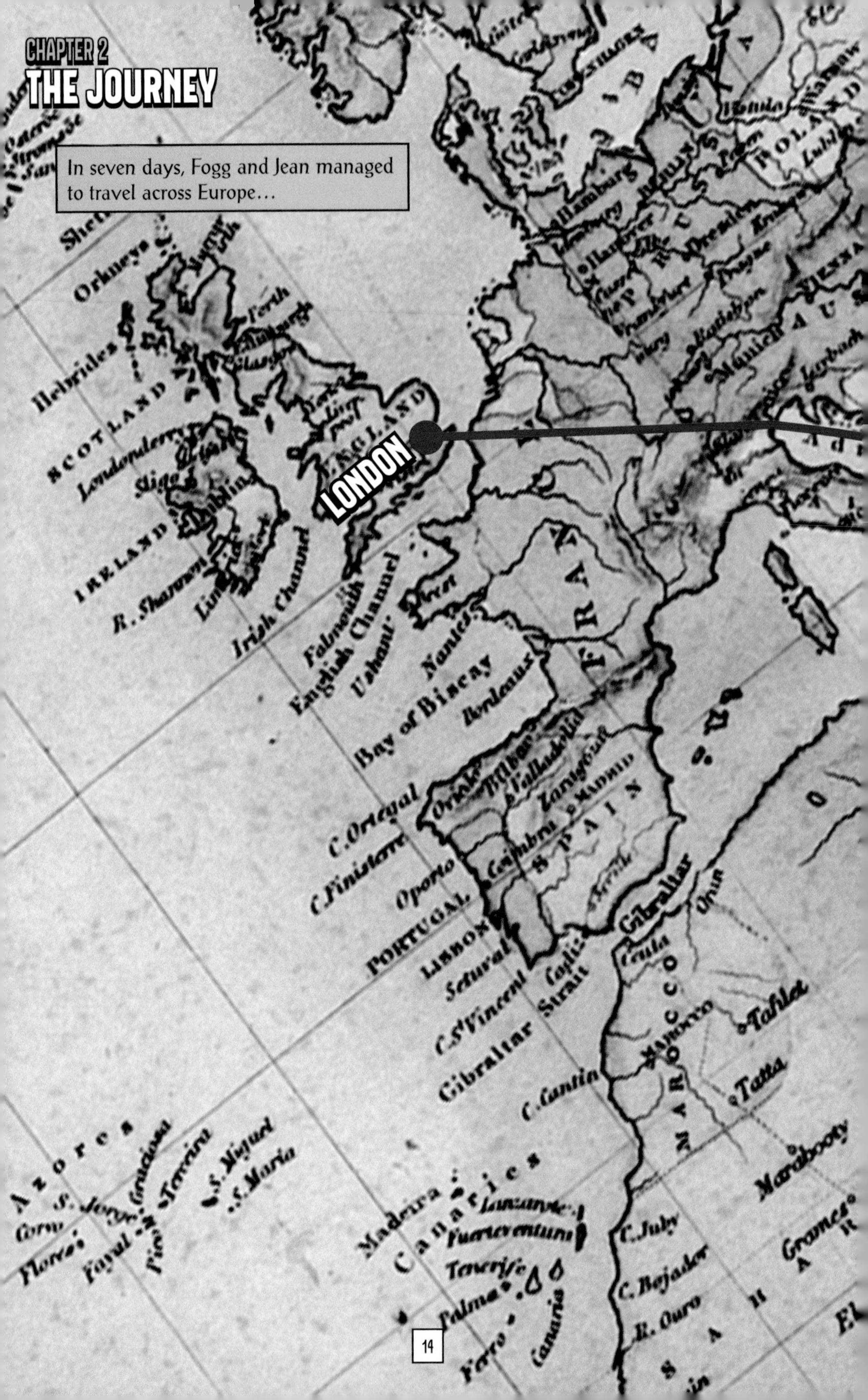

In seven days, Fogg and Jean managed to travel across Europe…
LONDON
Orkneys
Hebrides
SCOTLAND
Forth
Londonderry
Sligo
Dublin
IRELAND
R. Shannon
Irish Channel
ENGLAND
Liverpool
Falmouth
English Channel
Ushant
Brest
Nantes
Bay of Biscay
Bordeaux
Hamburg
Hanover
Dresden
Prague
C. Ortegal
C. Finisterre
Oporto
PORTUGAL
LISBON
Setuval
C. St Vincent
Cadiz
Strait
Gibraltar
Gibraltar
SPAIN
Valladolid
Zaragoza
Madrid
Coimbra
Ceuta
Oran
Tafilet
Tatta
C. Cantin
C. Juby
C. Bojador
R. Ouro
Azores
Flores
Corvo
S. Jorge
Fayal
Pico
Graciosa
Terceira
S. Miguel
S. Maria
Madeira
Canaries
Lanzarote
Fuerteventura
Teneriffe
Palma
Ferro
Canaria

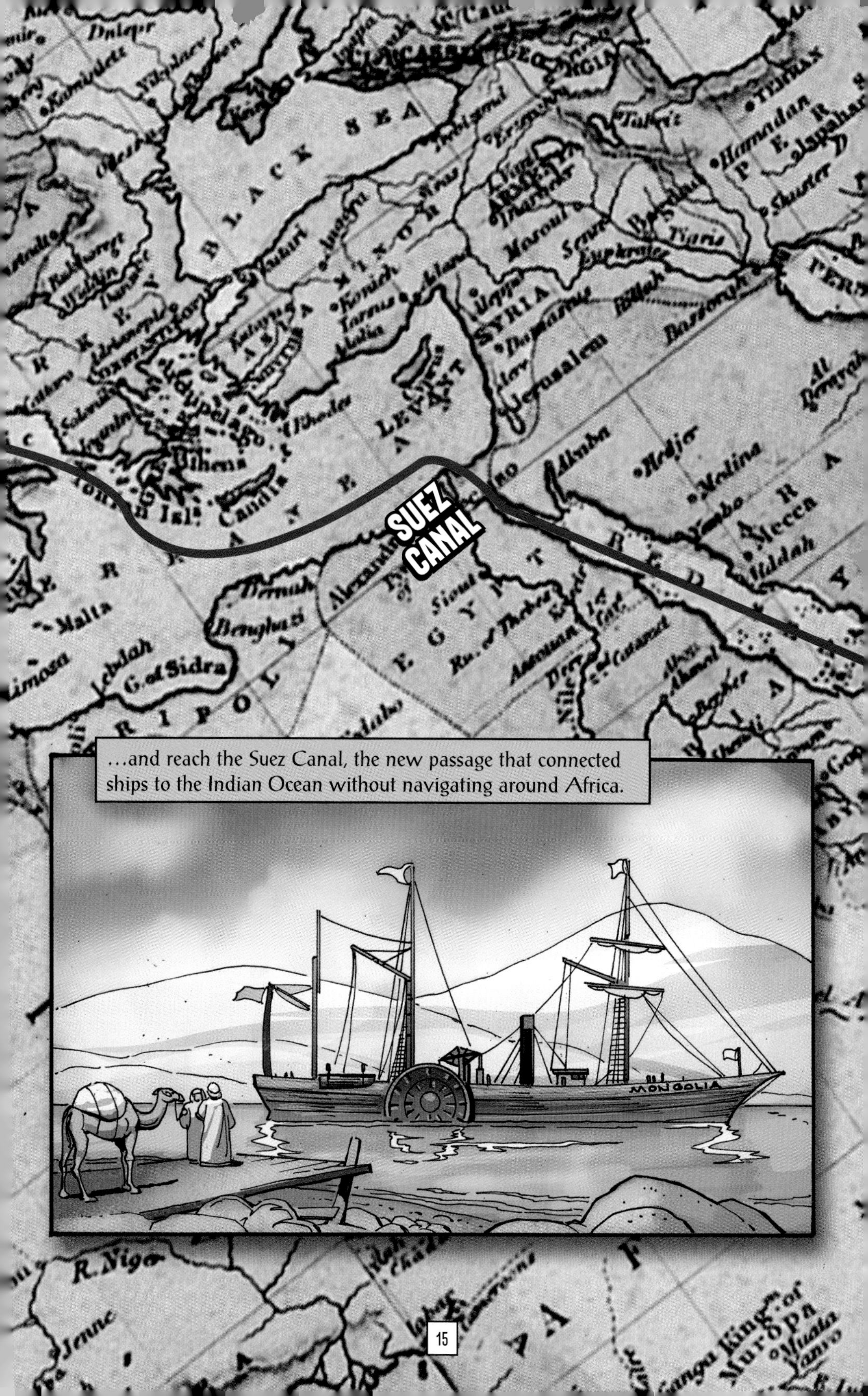
BLACK SEA
SYRIA
Jerusalem
Athens
Malta
Medina
Mecca
SUEZ CANAL
...and reach the Suez Canal, the new passage that connected ships to the Indian Ocean without navigating around Africa.
MONGOLIA
R. Niger

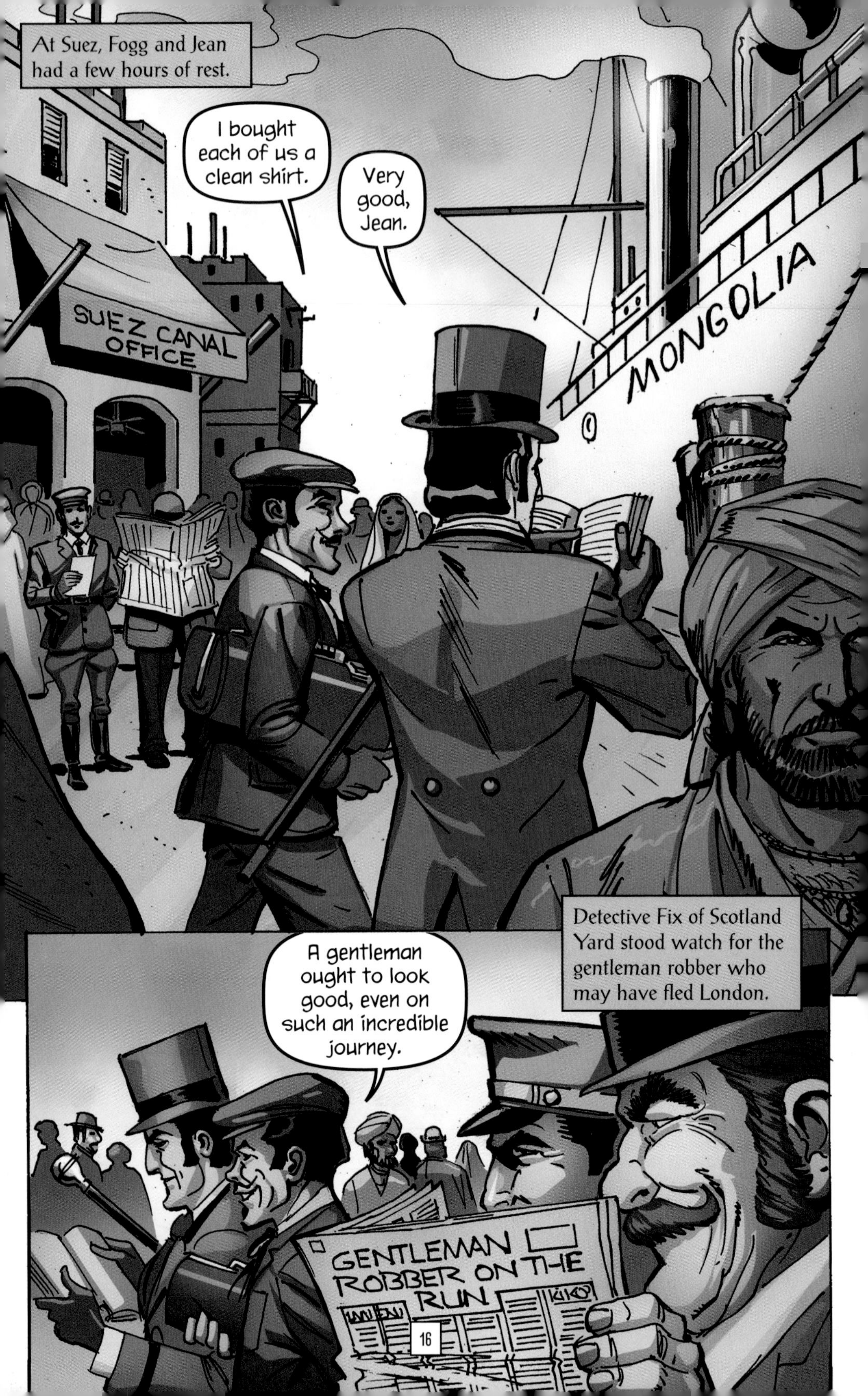
At Suez, Fogg and Jean had a few hours of rest.
I bought each of us a clean shirt.
Very good, Jean.
SUEZ CANAL OFFICE
MONGOLIA
Detective Fix of Scotland Yard stood watch for the gentleman robber who may have fled London.
A gentleman ought to look good, even on such an incredible journey.
GENTLEMAN ROBBER ON THE RUN

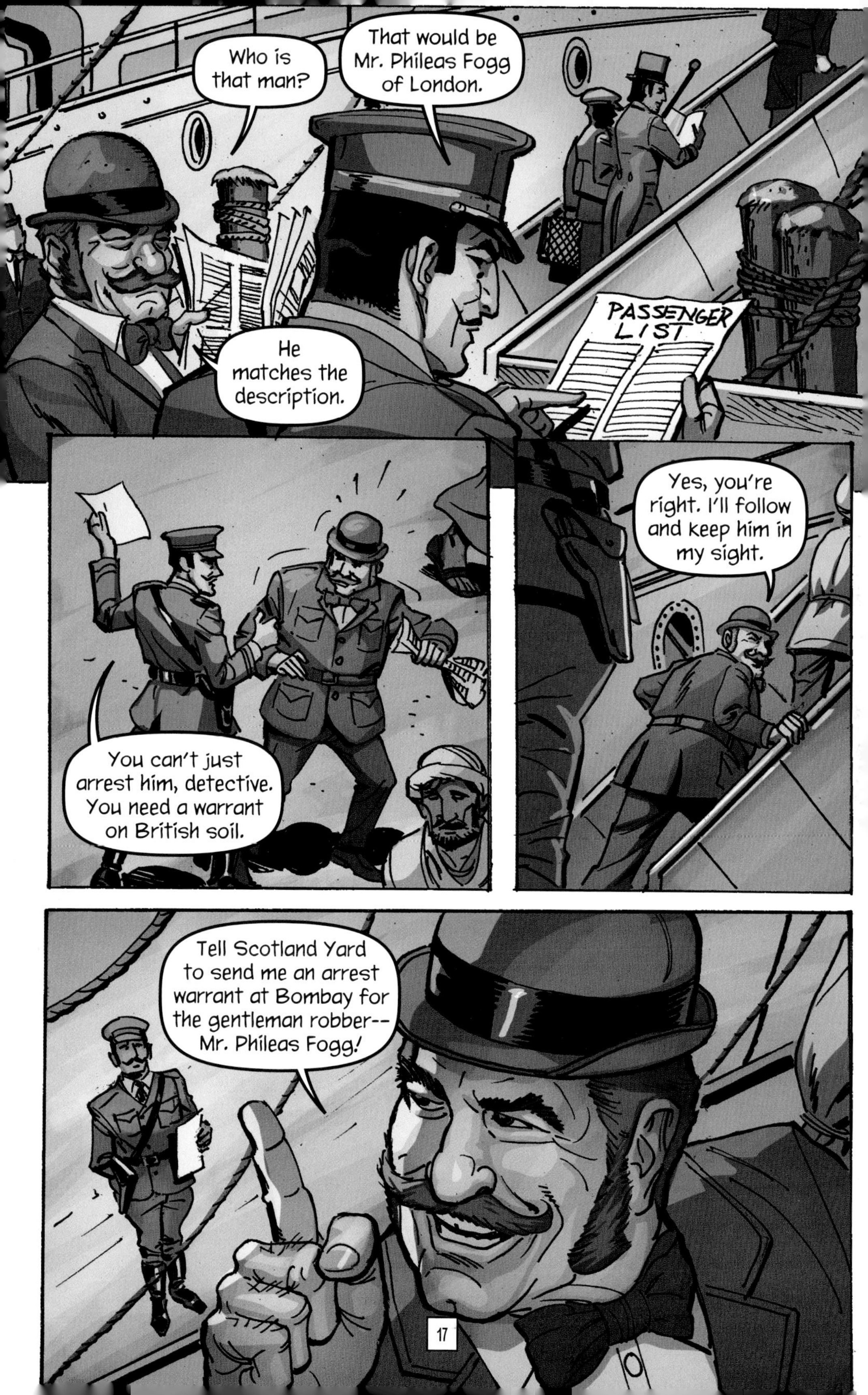
Who is that man?
That would be Mr. Phileas Fogg of London.
PASSENGER LIST
He matches the description.
You can't just arrest him, detective. You need a warrant on British soil.
Yes, you're right. I'll follow and keep him in my sight.
Tell Scotland Yard to send me an arrest warrant at Bombay for the gentleman robber-- Mr. Phileas Fogg!

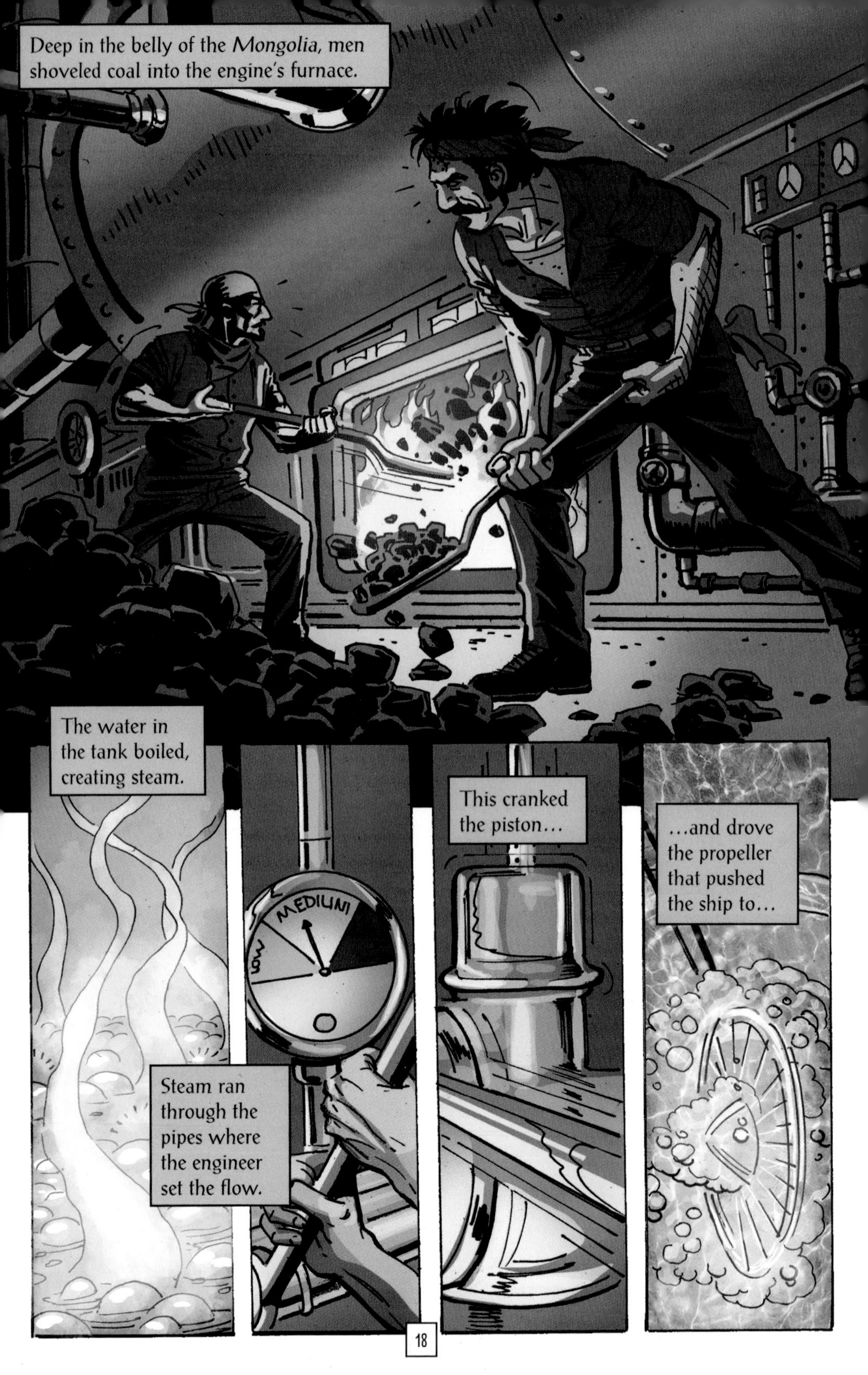
Deep in the belly of the *Mongolia,* men shoveled coal into the engine's furnace.
The water in the tank boiled, creating steam.
Steam ran through the pipes where the engineer set the flow.
LOW
MEDIUM
This cranked the piston...
...and drove the propeller that pushed the ship to...

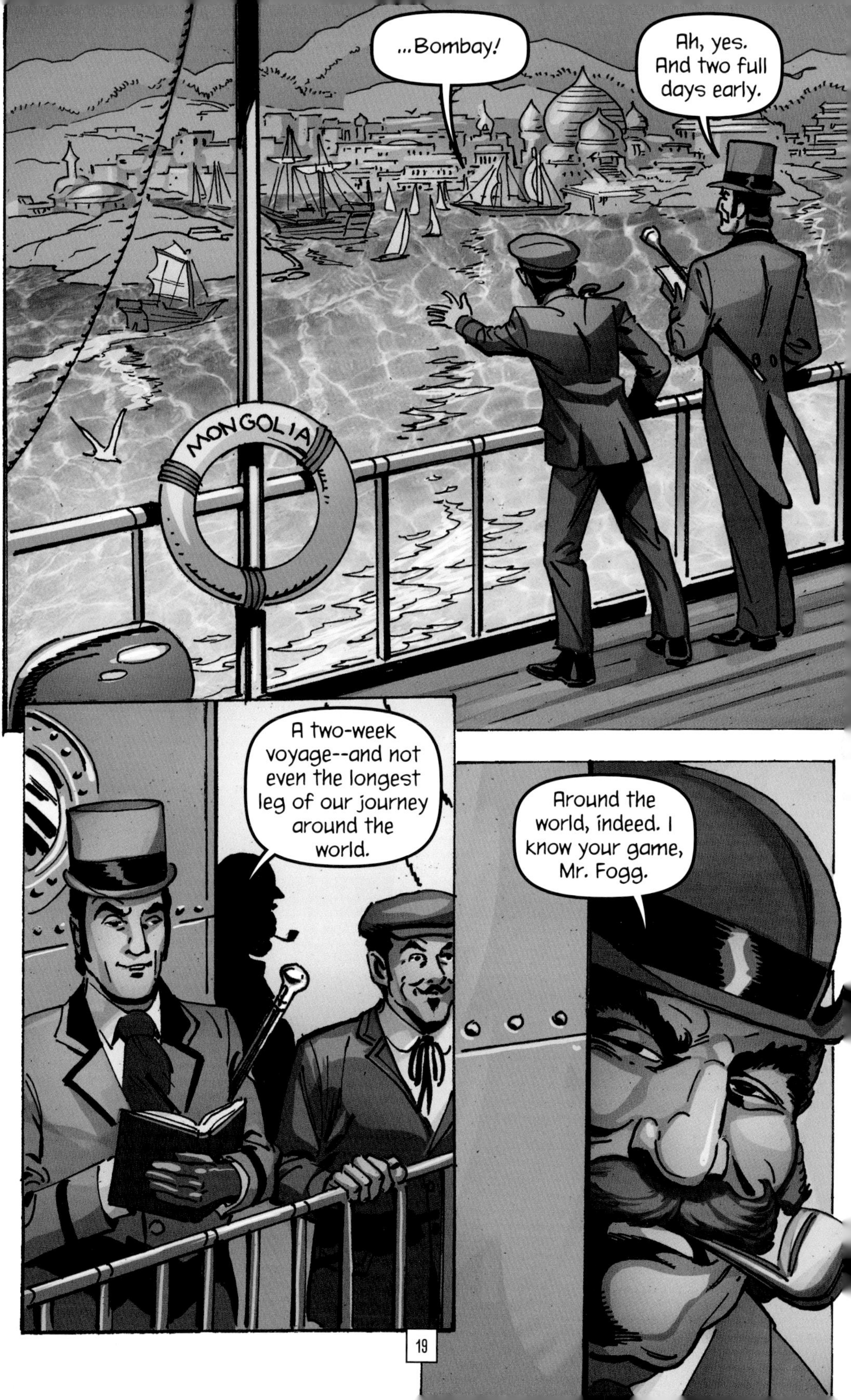
...Bombay!
Ah, yes. And two full days early.
MONGOLIA
A two-week voyage--and not even the longest leg of our journey around the world.
Around the world, indeed. I know your game, Mr. Fogg.

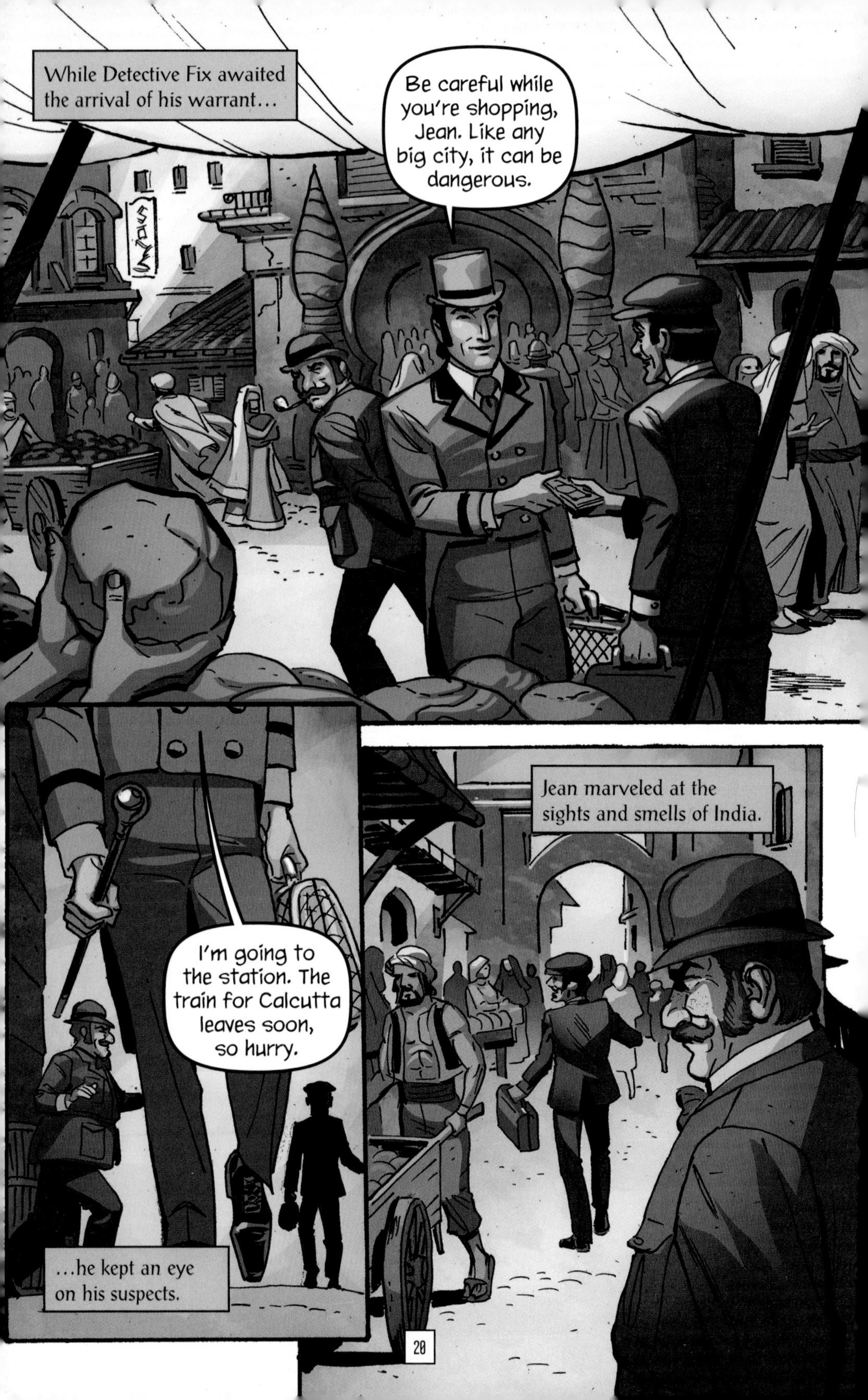
While Detective Fix awaited the arrival of his warrant...
Be careful while you're shopping, Jean. Like any big city, it can be dangerous.
I'm going to the station. The train for Calcutta leaves soon, so hurry.
...he kept an eye on his suspects.
Jean marveled at the sights and smells of India.

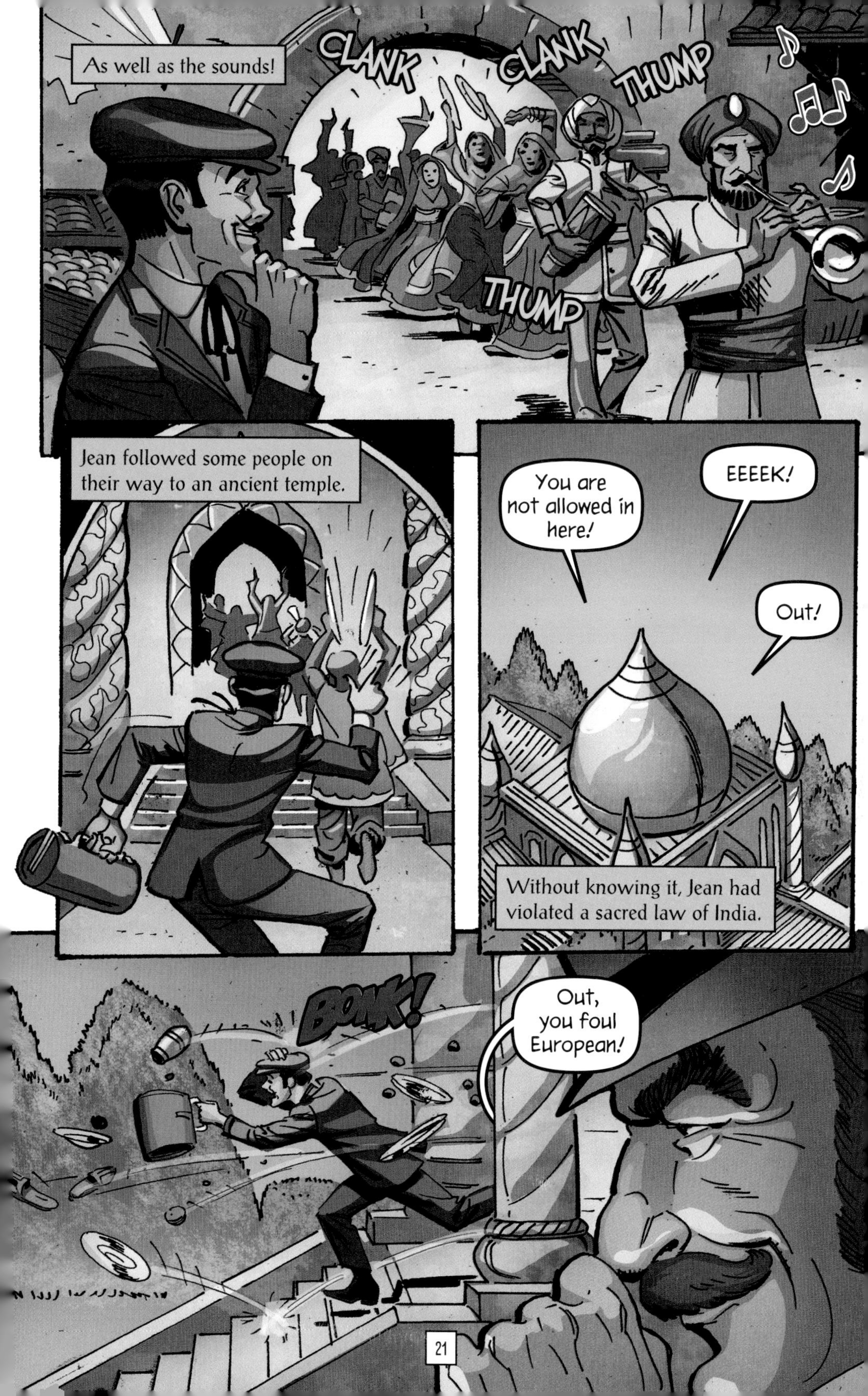
As well as the sounds!
CLANK
CLANK
THUMP
THUMP
Jean followed some people on their way to an ancient temple.
You are not allowed in here!
EEEEK!
Out!
Without knowing it, Jean had violated a sacred law of India.
BONK!
Out, you foul European!

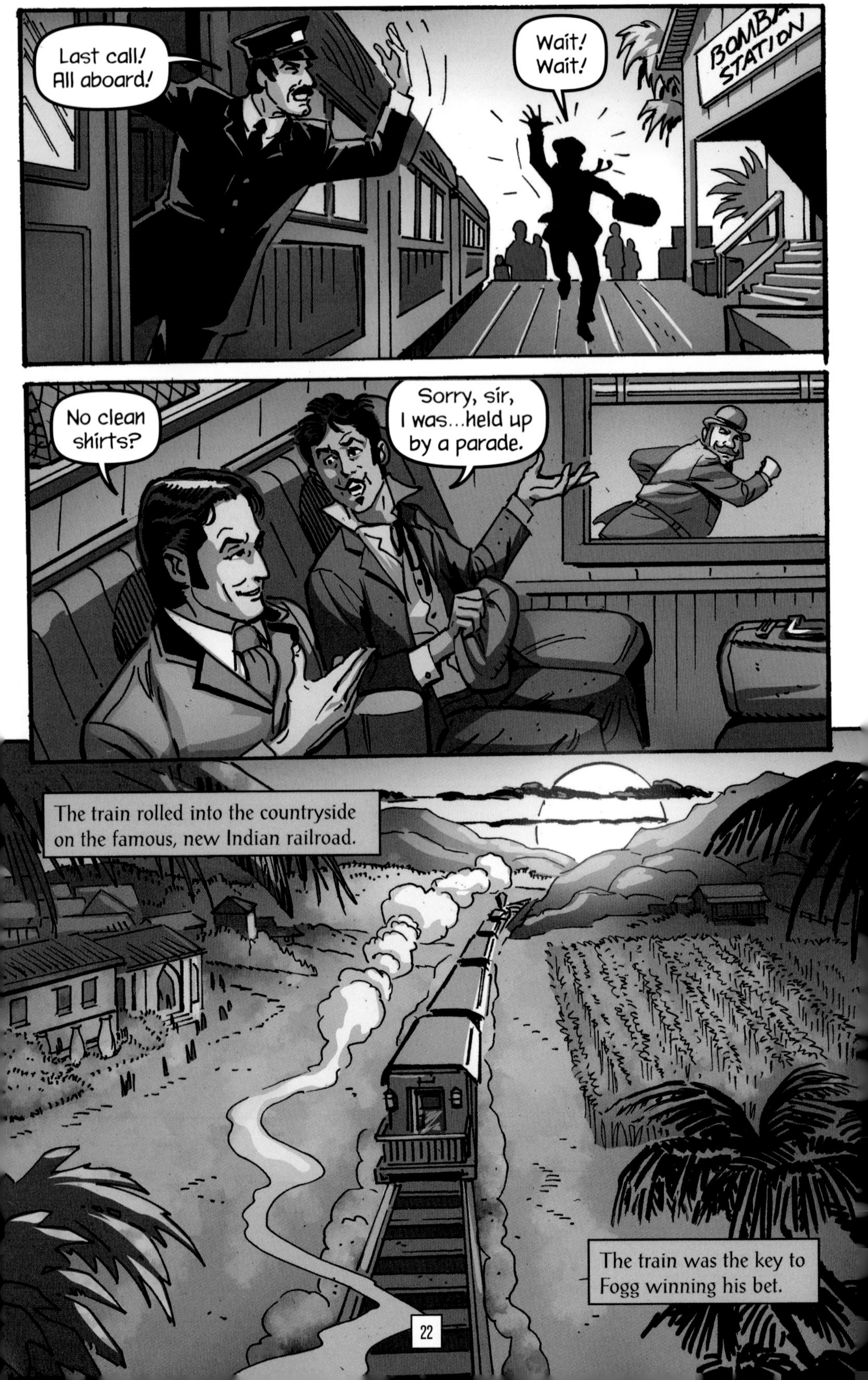
Last call! All aboard!
Wait! Wait!
BOMBA STATION
No clean shirts?
Sorry, sir, I was…held up by a parade.
The train rolled into the countryside on the famous, new Indian railroad.
The train was the key to Fogg winning his bet.

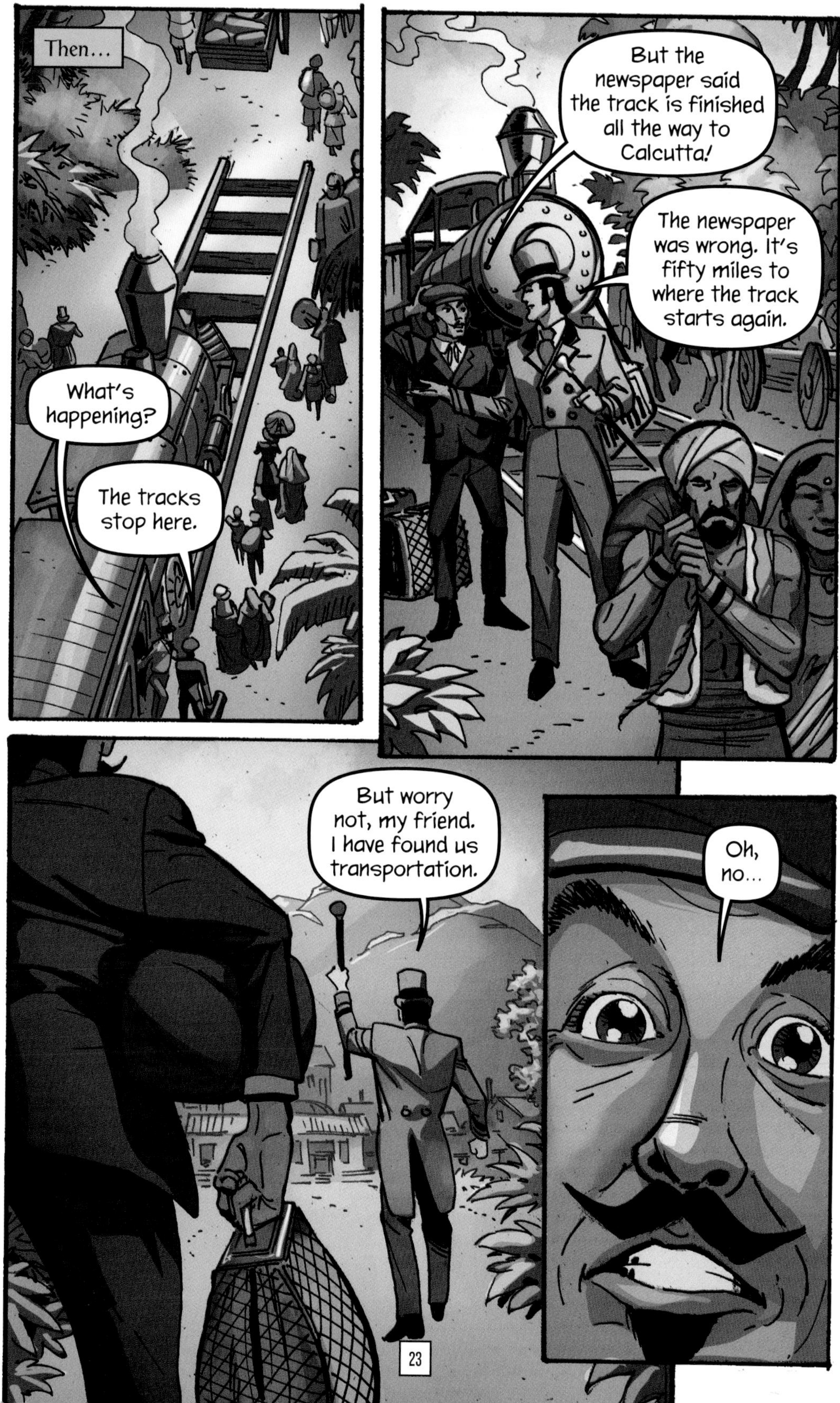
Then...
What's happening?
The tracks stop here.
But the newspaper said the track is finished all the way to Calcutta!
The newspaper was wrong. It's fifty miles to where the track starts again.
But worry not, my friend. I have found us transportation.
Oh, no...

CHAPTER 3
AOUDA

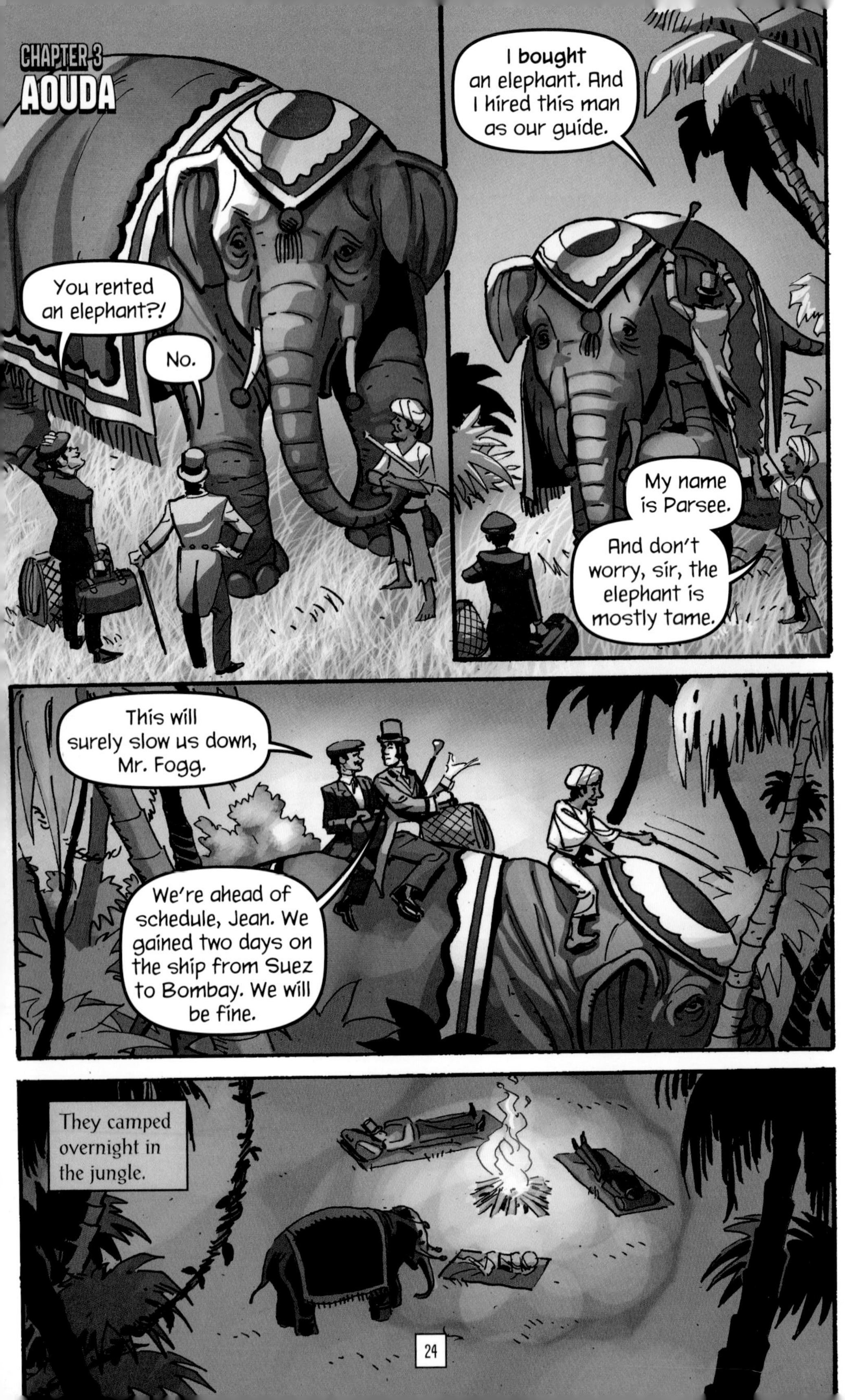
You rented an elephant?!
No.
I bought an elephant. And I hired this man as our guide.
My name is Parsee.
And don't worry, sir, the elephant is mostly tame.
This will surely slow us down, Mr. Fogg.
We're ahead of schedule, Jean. We gained two days on the ship from Suez to Bombay. We will be fine.
They camped overnight in the jungle.

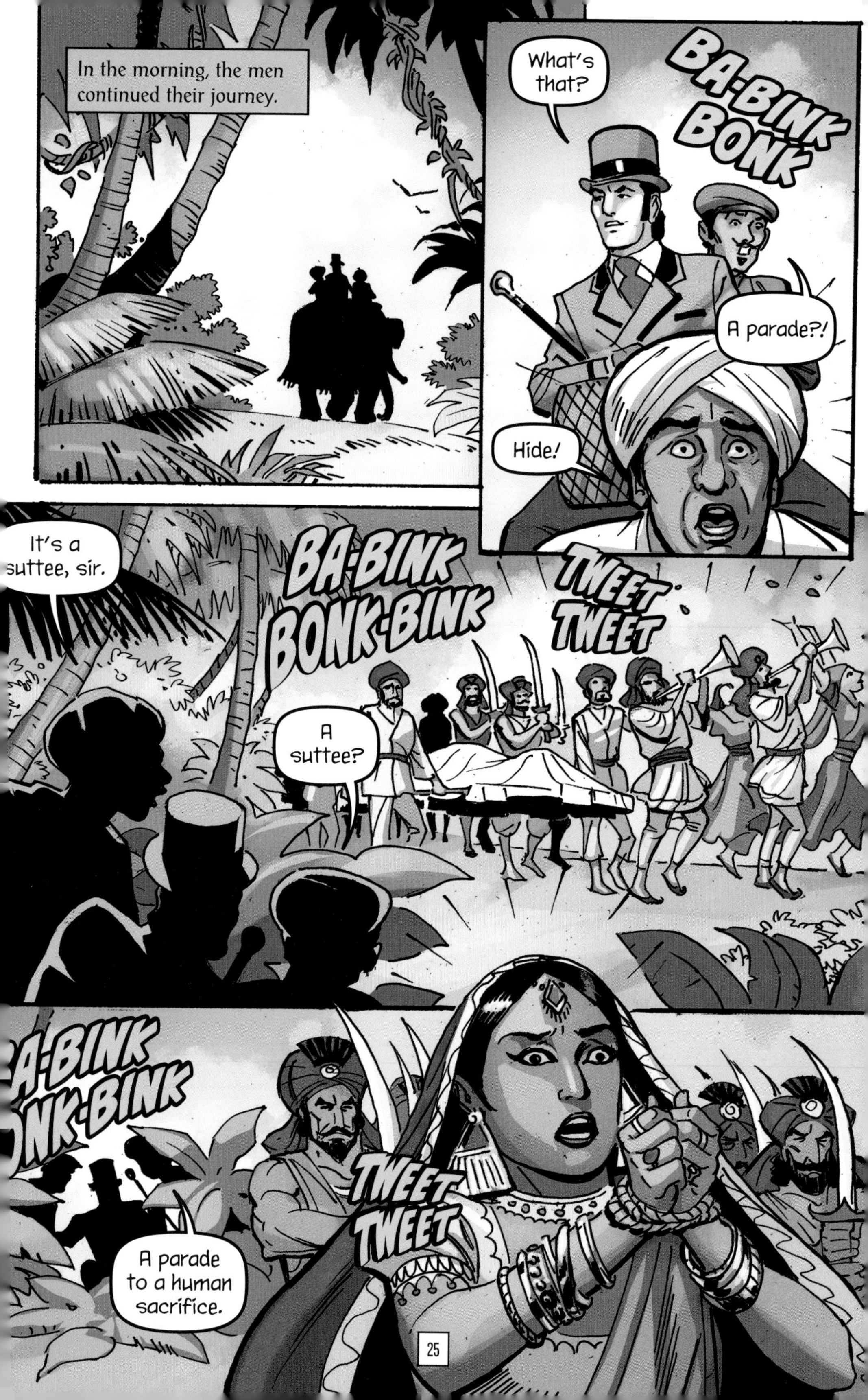

In the morning, the men continued their journey.
What's that?
BA-BINK BONK
A parade?!
Hide!
It's a suttee, sir.
BA-BINK BONK-BINK
TWEET TWEET
A suttee?
A parade to a human sacrifice.
TWEET TWEET

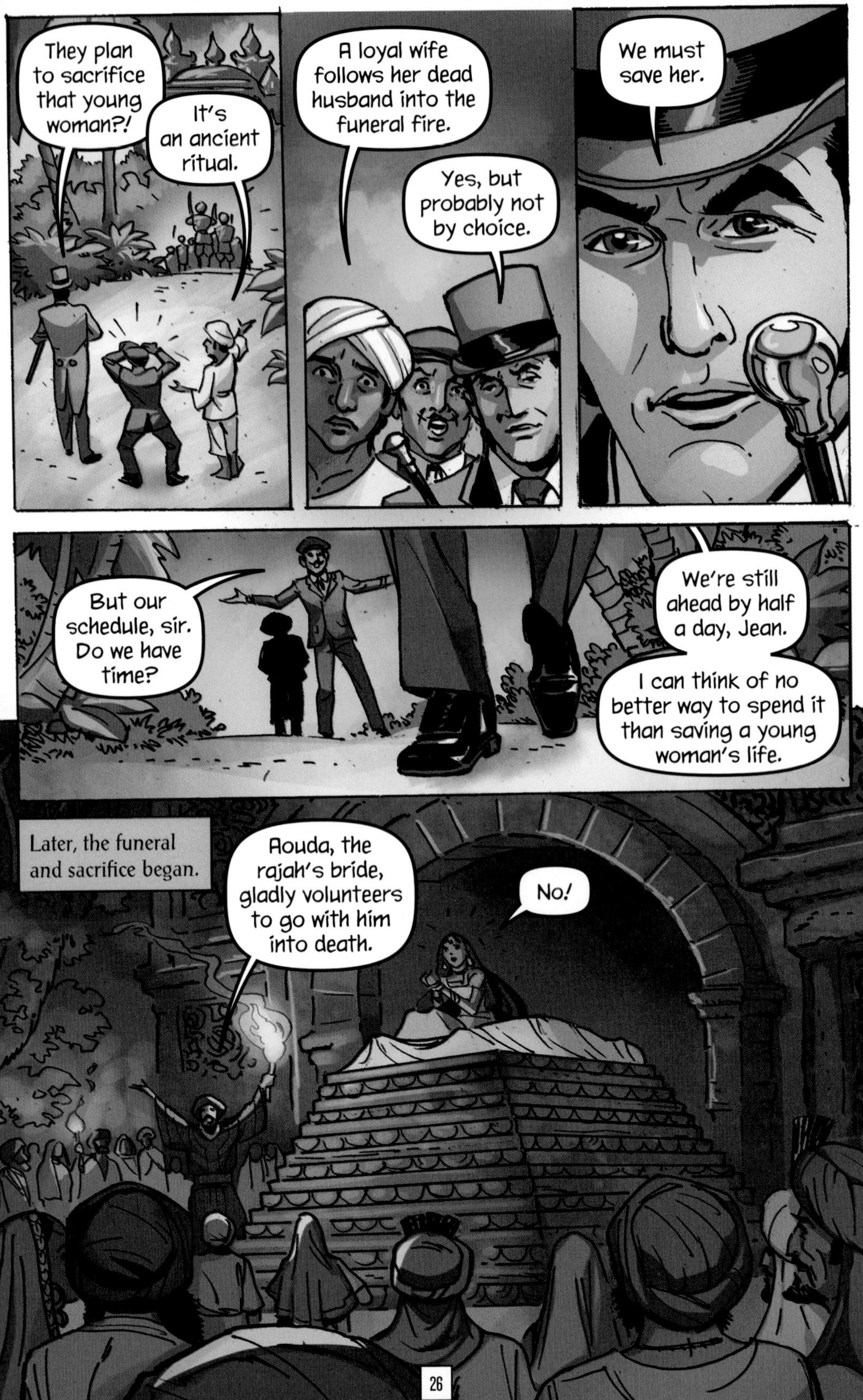
They plan to sacrifice that young woman?!
It's an ancient ritual.
A loyal wife follows her dead husband into the funeral fire.
Yes, but probably not by choice.
We must save her.
But our schedule, sir. Do we have time?
We're still ahead by half a day, Jean.
I can think of no better way to spend it than saving a young woman's life.
Later, the funeral and sacrifice began.
Aouda, the rajah's bride, gladly volunteers to go with him into death.
No!

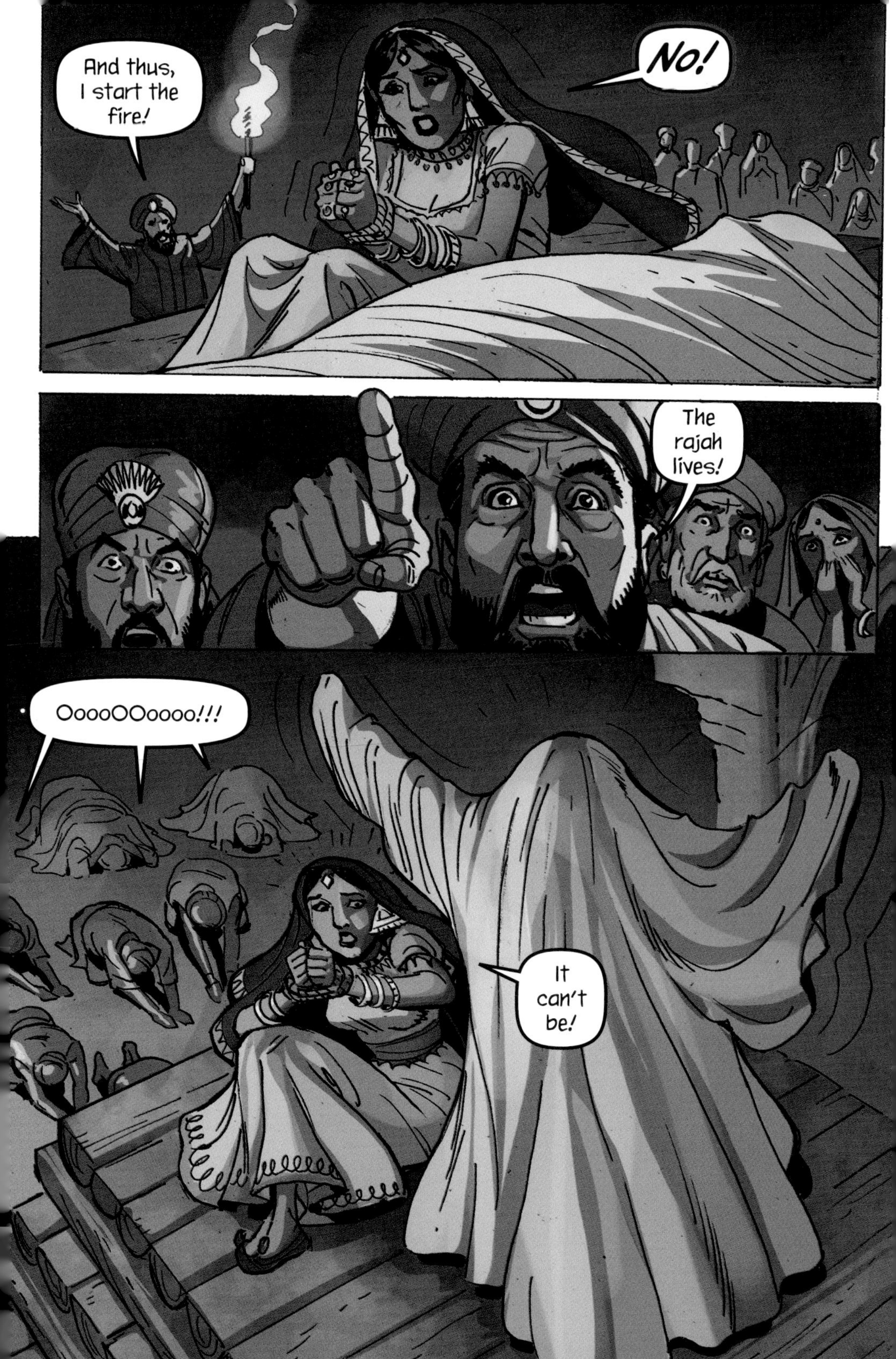
And thus, I start the fire!
No!
The rajah lives!
OoooOOoooo!!!
It can't be!

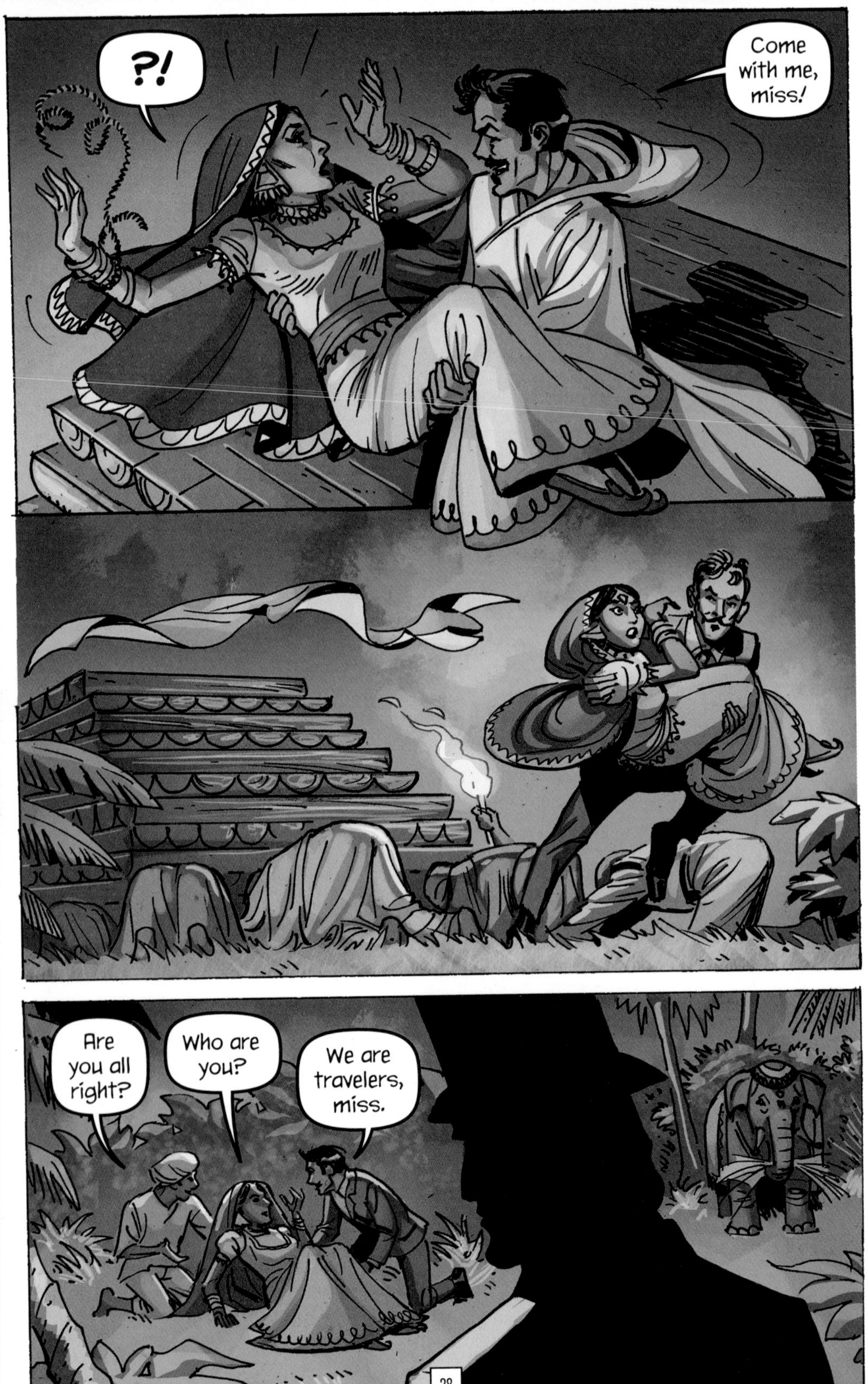
?!
Come with me, miss!
Are you all right?
Who are you?
We are travelers, miss.

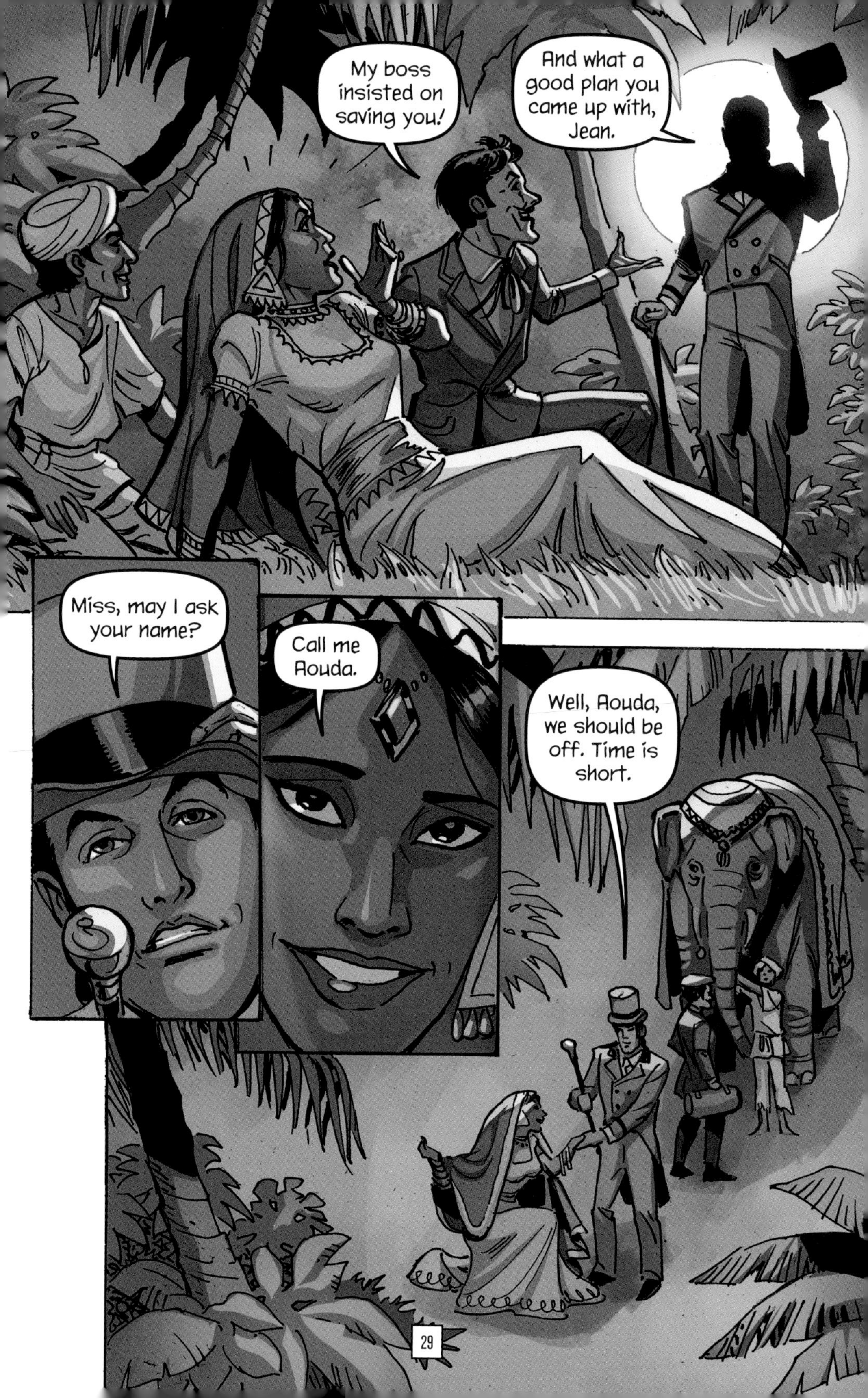
My boss insisted on saving you!
And what a good plan you came up with, Jean.
Miss, may I ask your name?
Call me Aouda.
Well, Aouda, we should be off. Time is short.

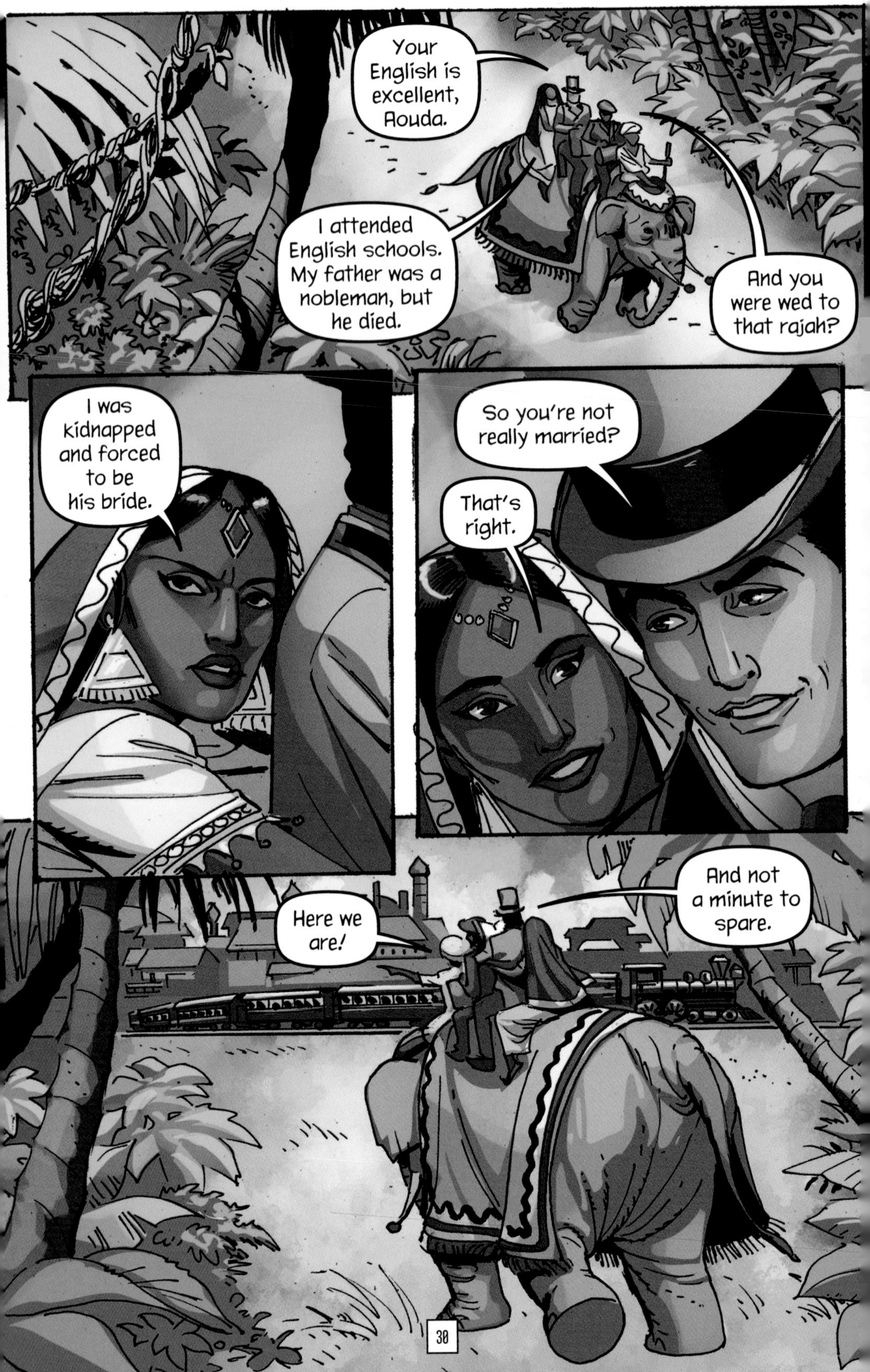
Your English is excellent, Aouda.
I attended English schools. My father was a nobleman, but he died.
And you were wed to that rajah?
I was kidnapped and forced to be his bride.
So you're not really married?
That's right.
Here we are!
And not a minute to spare.

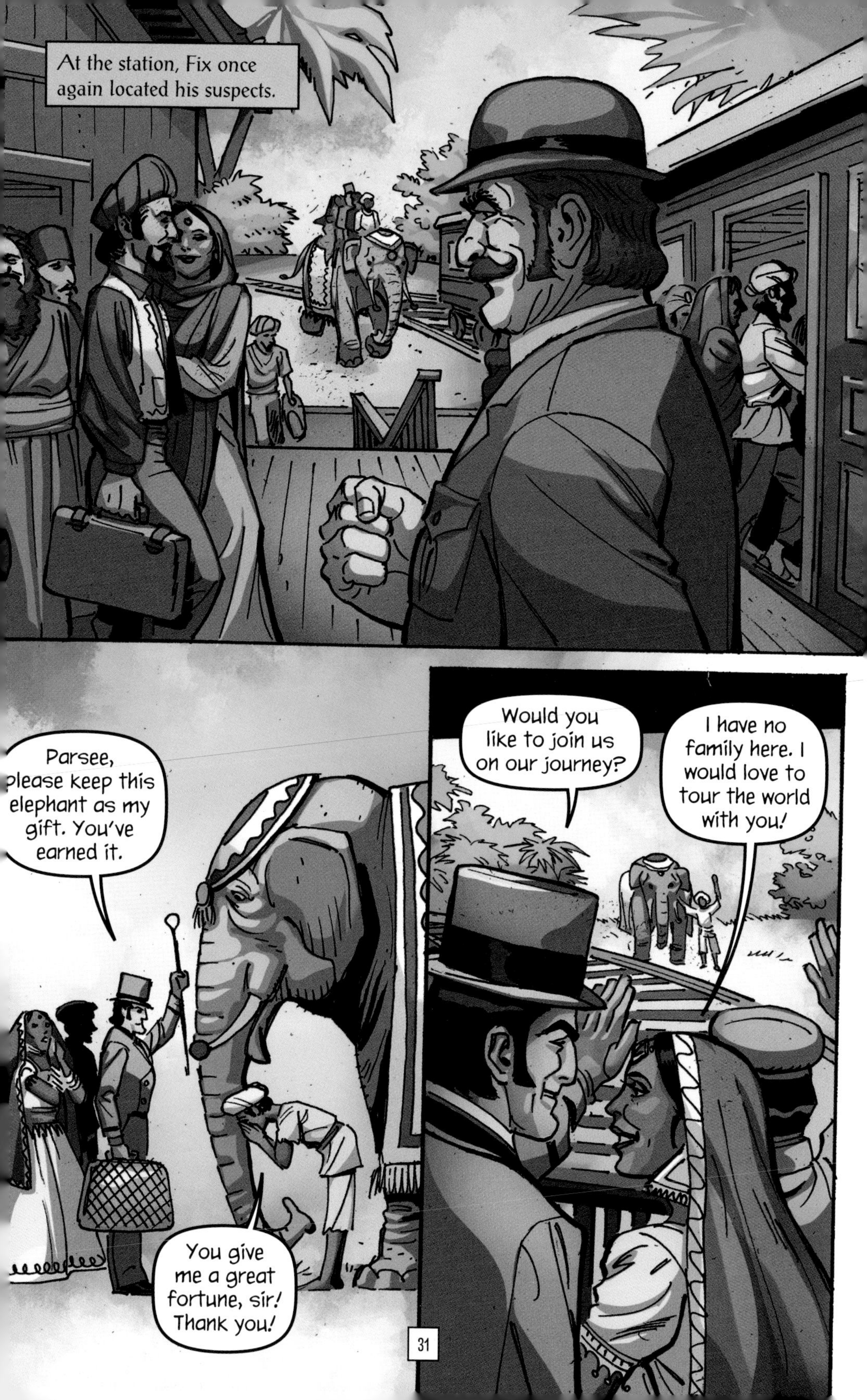
At the station, Fix once again located his suspects.
Parsee, please keep this elephant as my gift. You've earned it.
You give me a great fortune, sir! Thank you!
Would you like to join us on our journey?
I have no family here. I would love to tour the world with you!

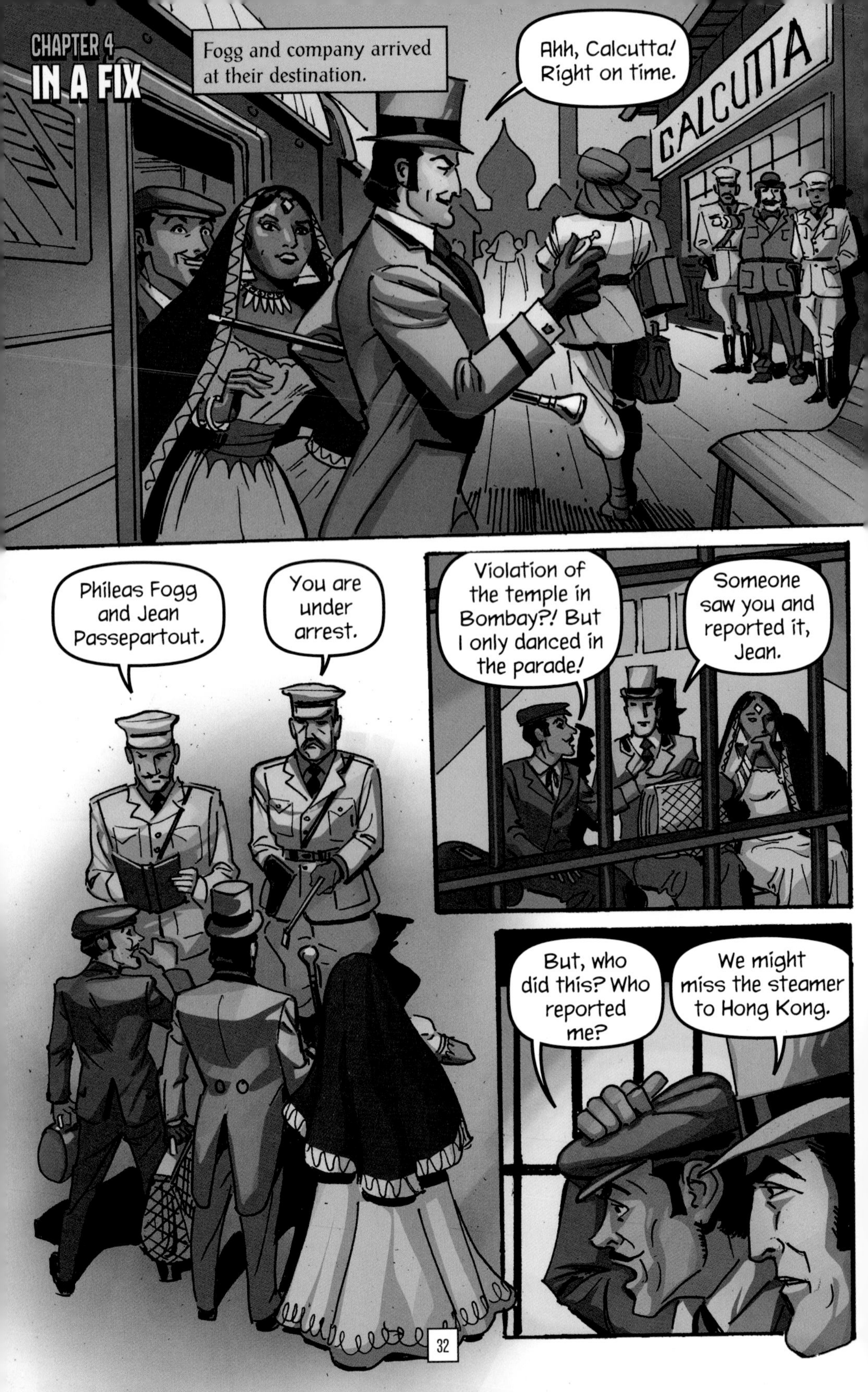
CHAPTER 4
IN A FIX
Fogg and company arrived at their destination.
Ahh, Calcutta! Right on time.
CALCUTTA
Phileas Fogg and Jean Passepartout.
You are under arrest.
Violation of the temple in Bombay?! But I only danced in the parade!
Someone saw you and reported it, Jean.
But, who did this? Who reported me?
We might miss the steamer to Hong Kong.

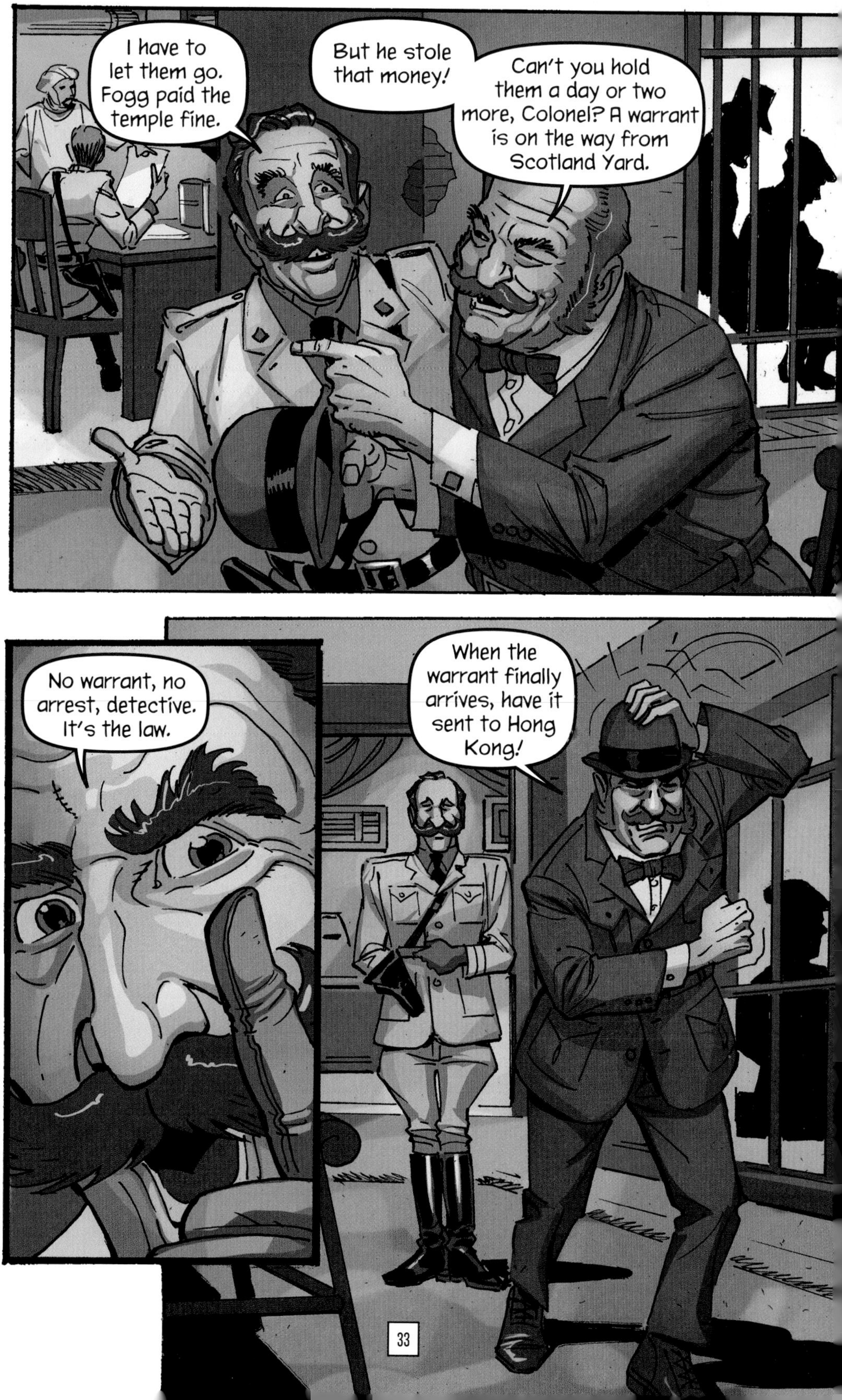
I have to let them go. Fogg paid the temple fine.
But he stole that money!
Can't you hold them a day or two more, Colonel? A warrant is on the way from Scotland Yard.
No warrant, no arrest, detective. It's the law.
When the warrant finally arrives, have it sent to Hong Kong!

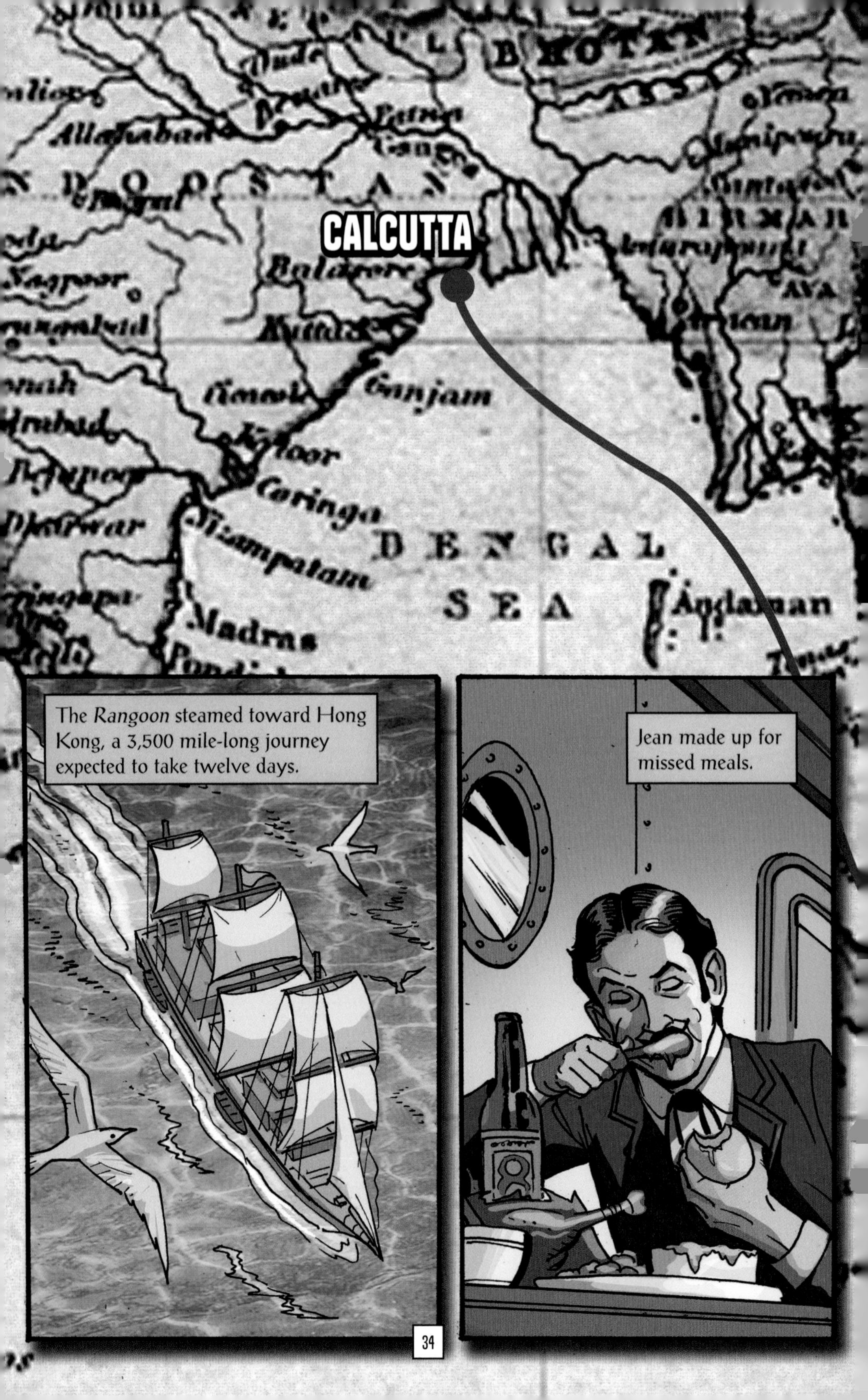
CALCUTTA
Allahabad
Ganjam
Coringa
BENGAL
SEA
Madras
Andaman
The *Rangoon* steamed toward Hong Kong, a 3,500 mile-long journey expected to take twelve days.
Jean made up for missed meals.

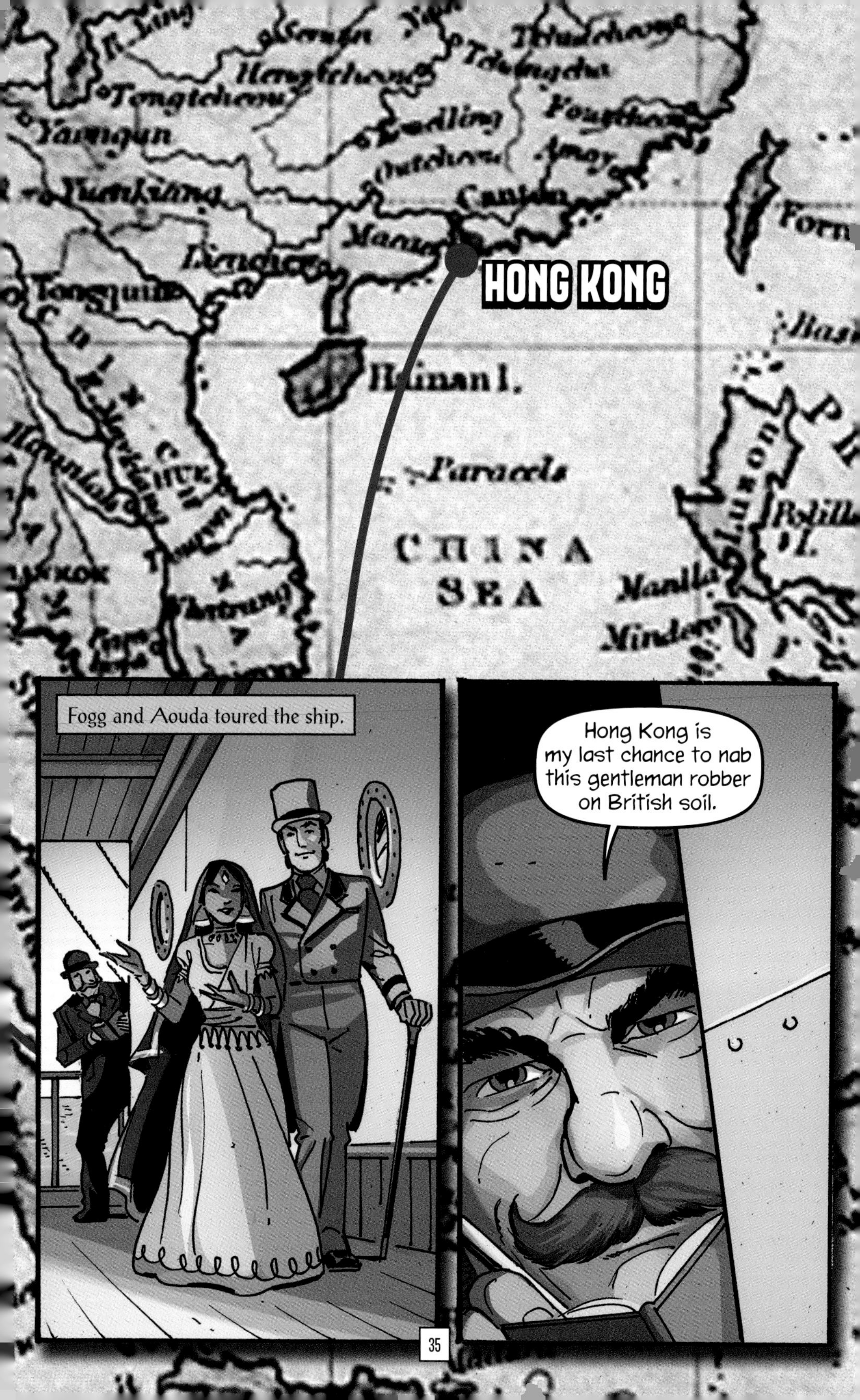

HONG KONG
Fogg and Aouda toured the ship.
Hong Kong is my last chance to nab this gentleman robber on British soil.

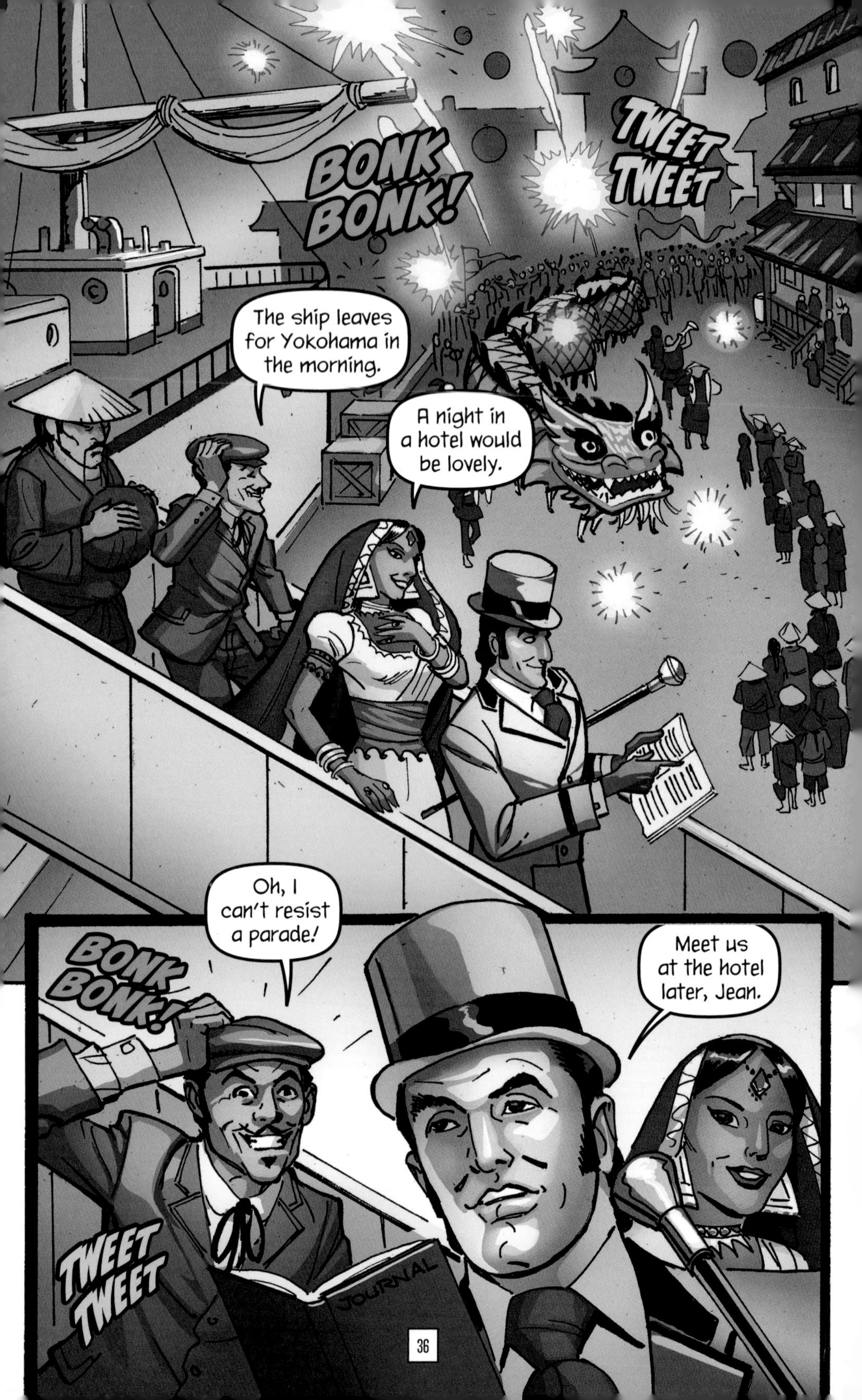
BONK BONK!
TWEET TWEET
The ship leaves for Yokohama in the morning.
A night in a hotel would be lovely.
Oh, I can't resist a parade!
BONK BONK!
Meet us at the hotel later, Jean.
TWEET TWEET
JOURNAL

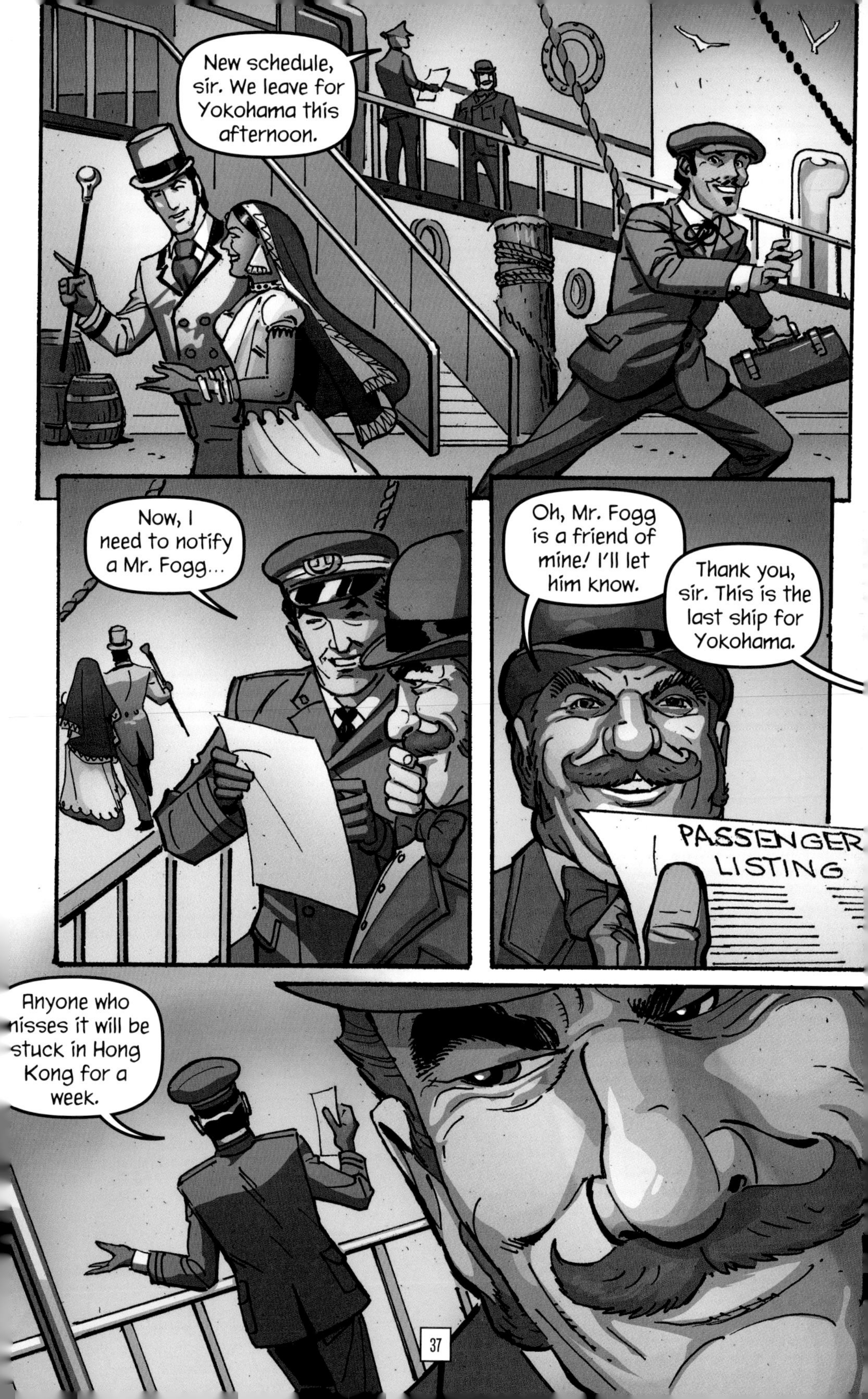

New schedule, sir. We leave for Yokohama this afternoon.
Now, I need to notify a Mr. Fogg...
Oh, Mr. Fogg is a friend of mine! I'll let him know.
Thank you, sir. This is the last ship for Yokohama.
PASSENGER LISTING
Anyone who misses it will be stuck in Hong Kong for a week.

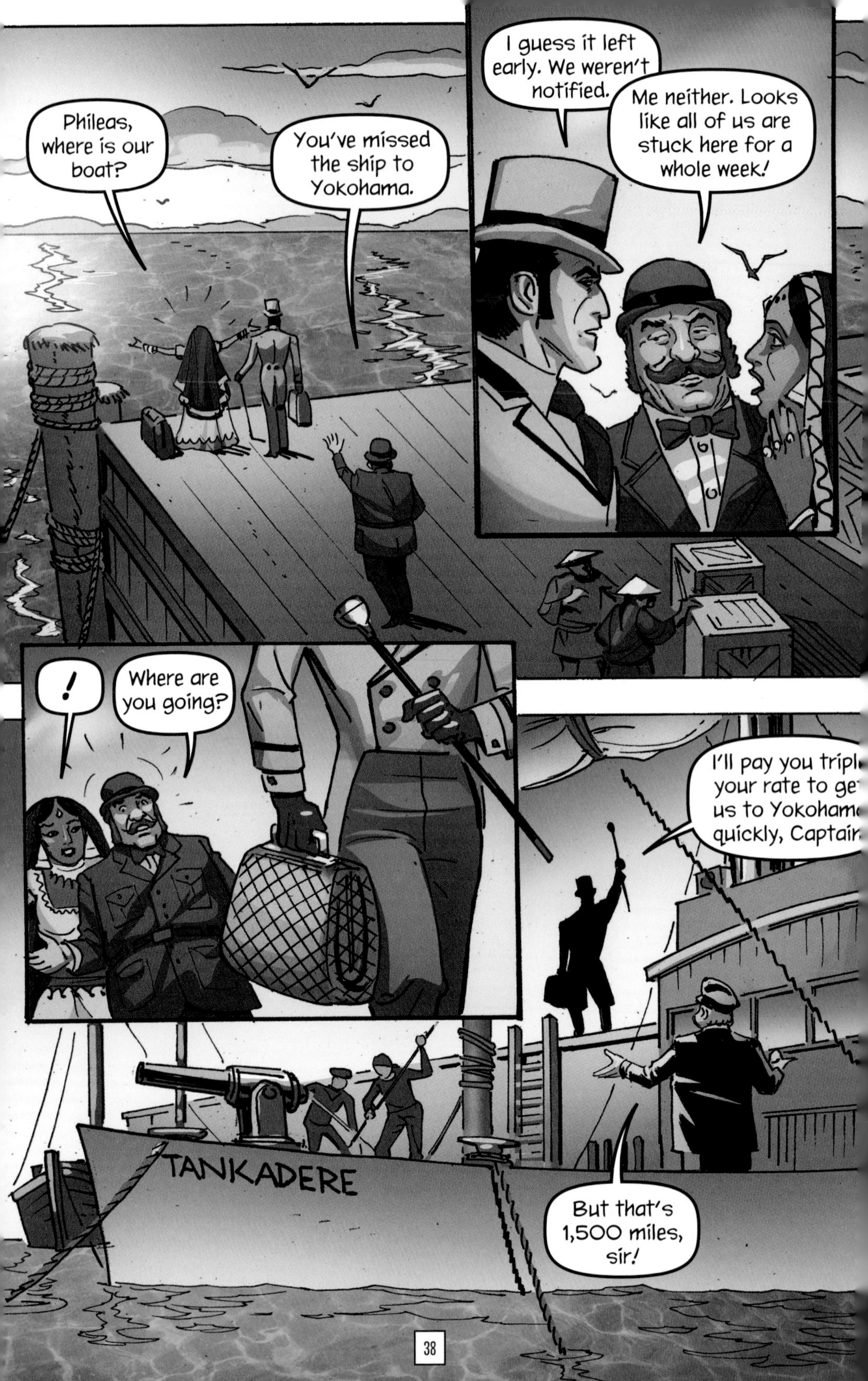
Phileas, where is our boat?
You've missed the ship to Yokohama.
I guess it left early. We weren't notified.
Me neither. Looks like all of us are stuck here for a whole week!
!
Where are you going?
I'll pay you tripl your rate to ge us to Yokoham quickly, Captai
TANKADERE
But that's 1,500 miles, sir!

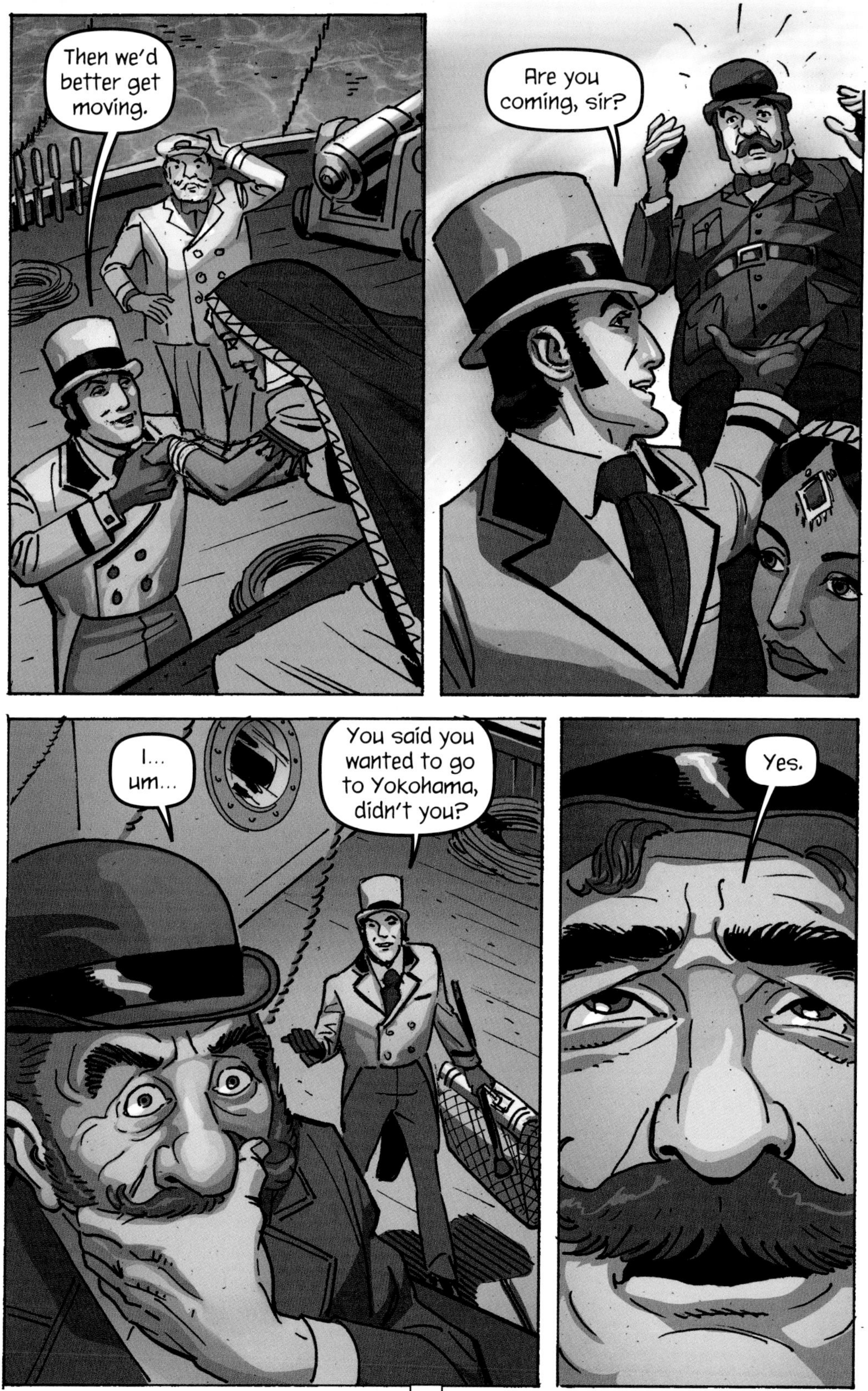
Then we'd better get moving.
Are you coming, sir?
I... um...
You said you wanted to go to Yokohama, didn't you?
Yes.

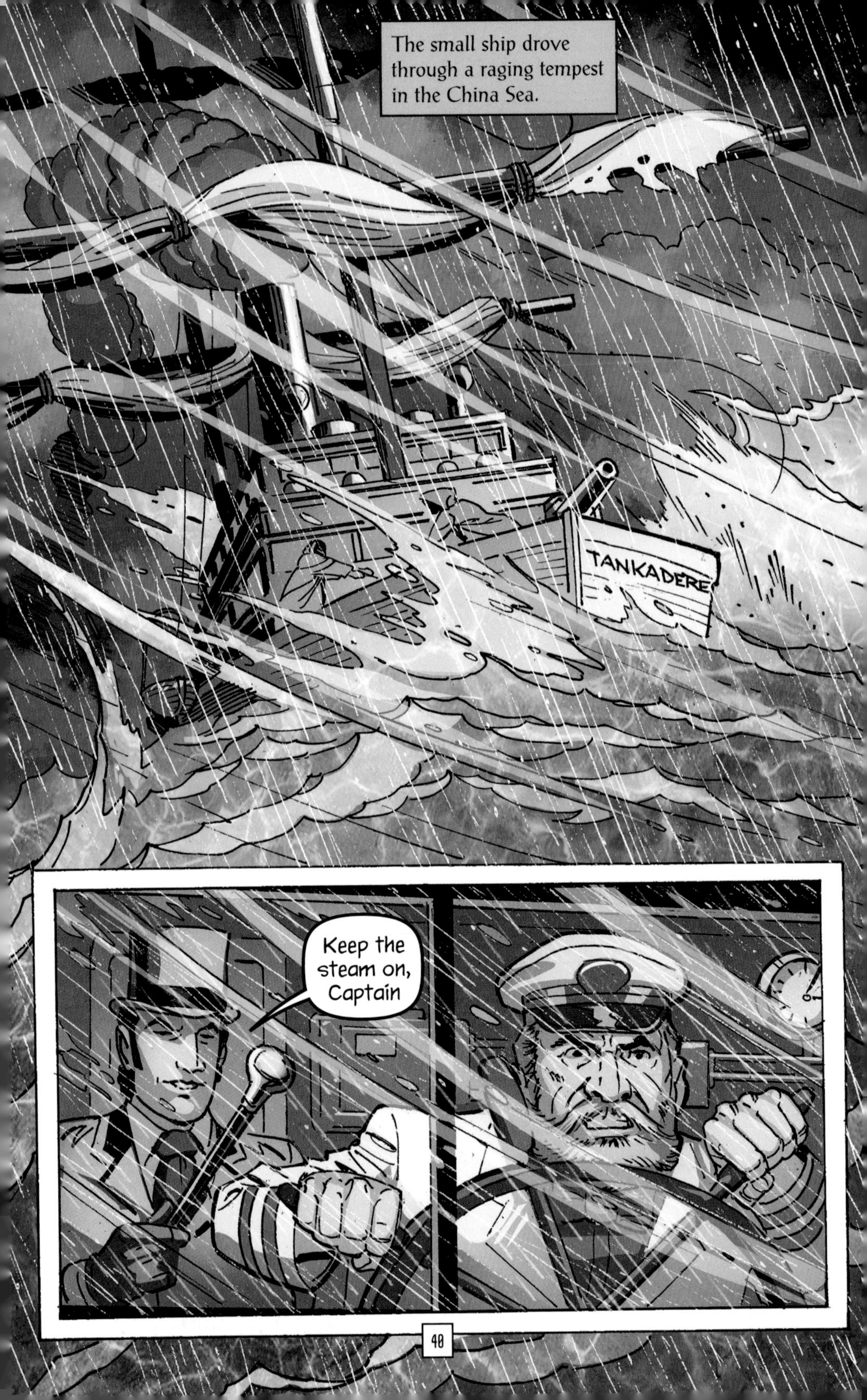
The small ship drove through a raging tempest in the China Sea.
TANKADERE
Keep the steam on, Captain

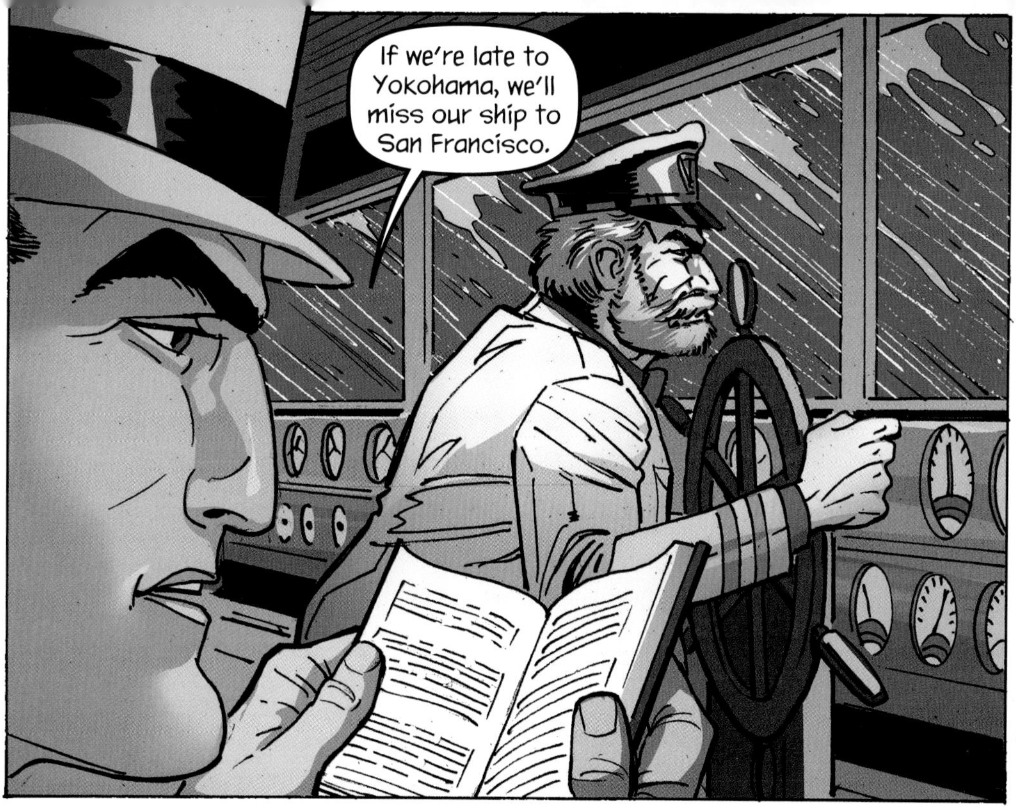
If we're late to Yokohama, we'll miss our ship to San Francisco.

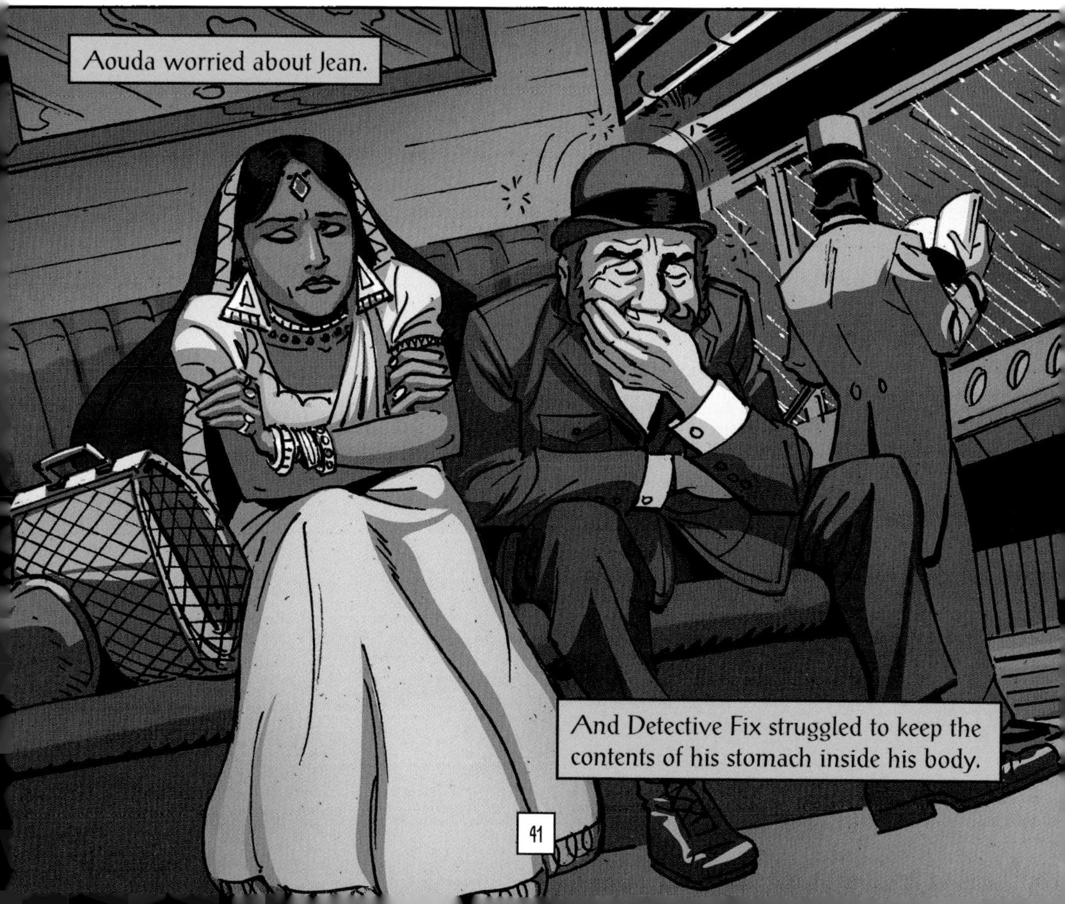
Aouda worried about Jean.
And Detective Fix struggled to keep the contents of his stomach inside his body.

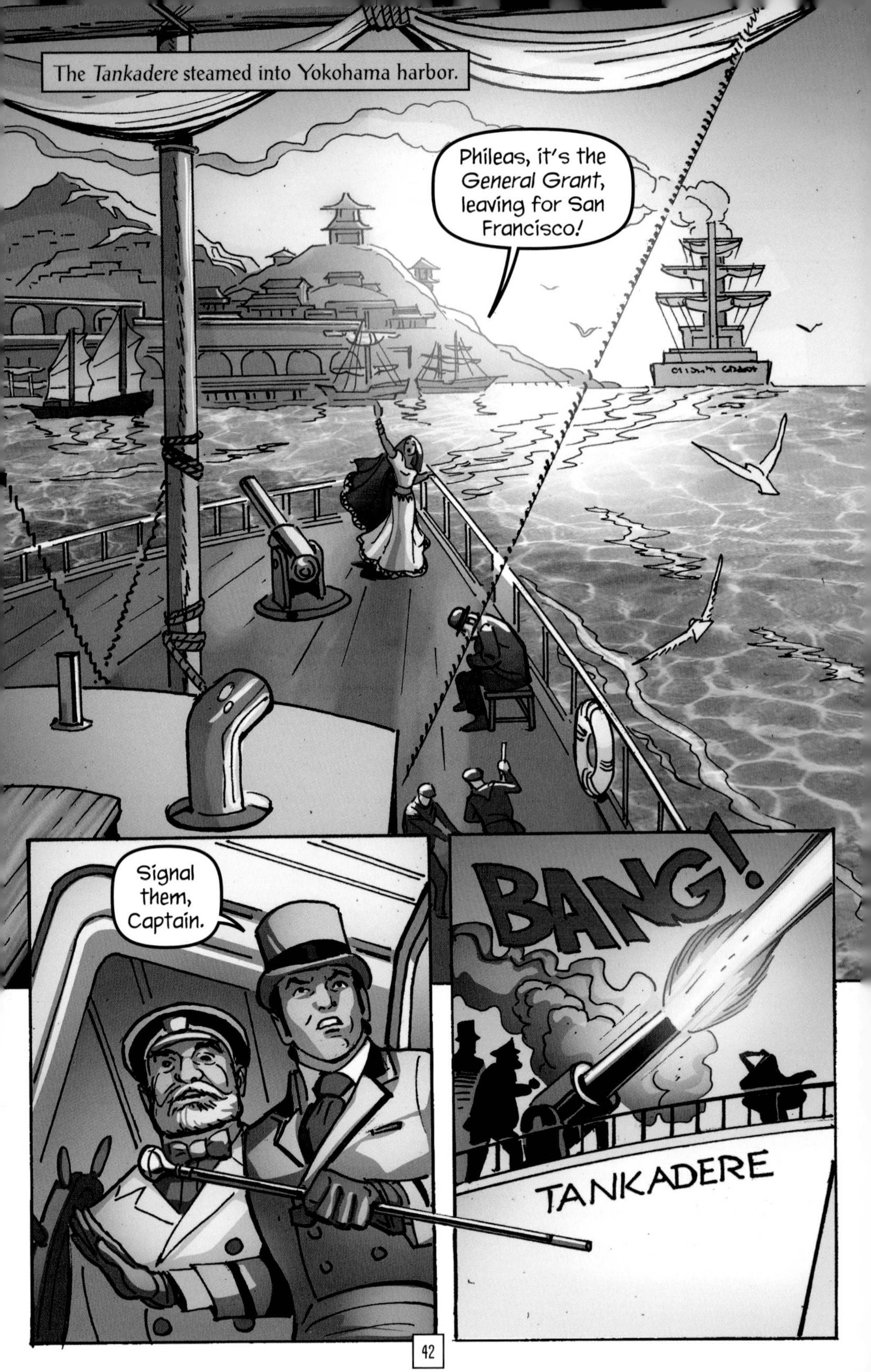
The *Tankadere* steamed into Yokohama harbor.
Phileas, it's the *General Grant*, leaving for San Francisco!
Signal them, Captain.
BANG!
TANKADERE

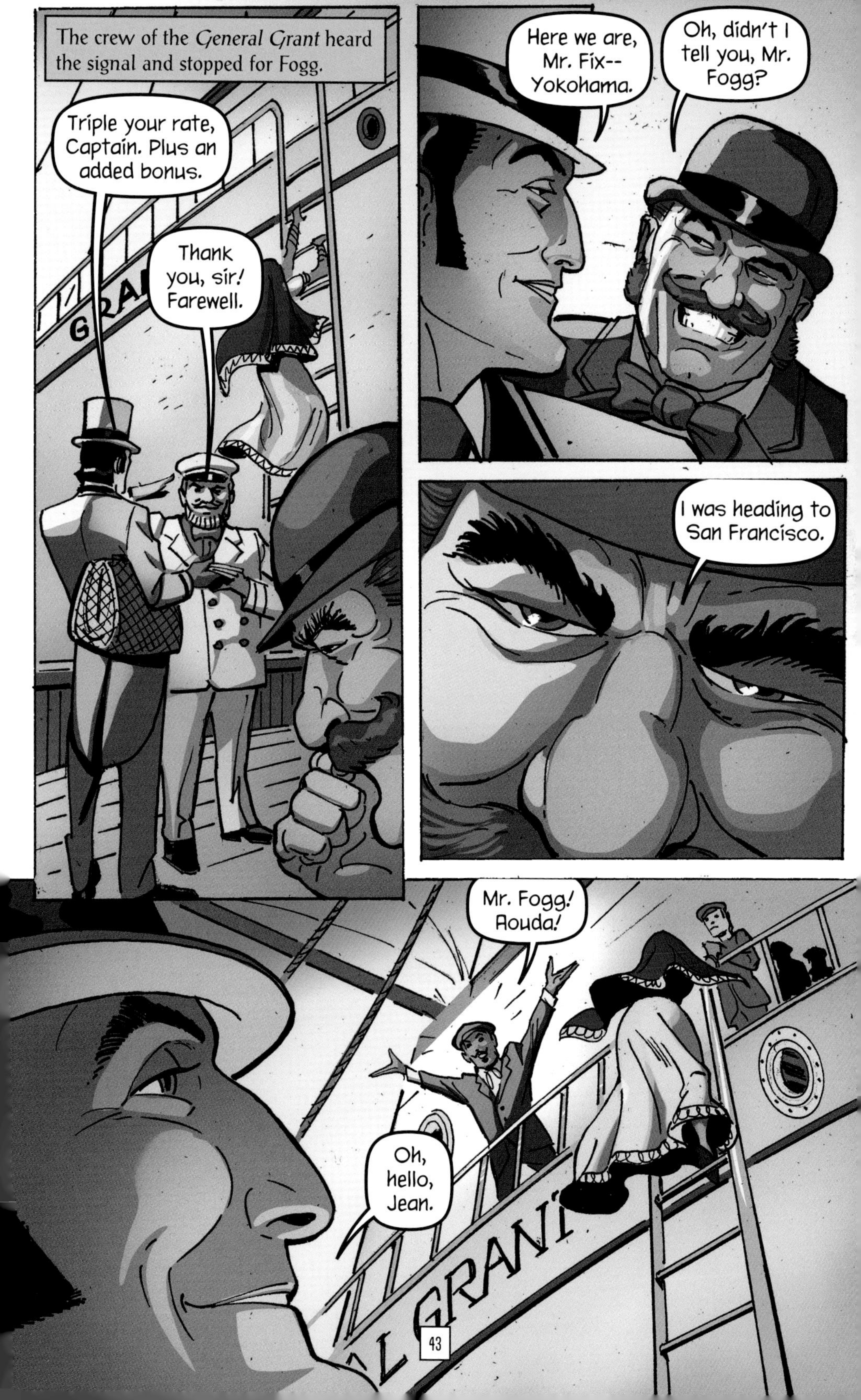
The crew of the *General Grant* heard the signal and stopped for Fogg.
Triple your rate, Captain. Plus an added bonus.
Thank you, sir! Farewell.
Here we are, Mr. Fix-- Yokohama.
Oh, didn't I tell you, Mr. Fogg?
I was heading to San Francisco.
Mr. Fogg! Aouda!
Oh, hello, Jean.

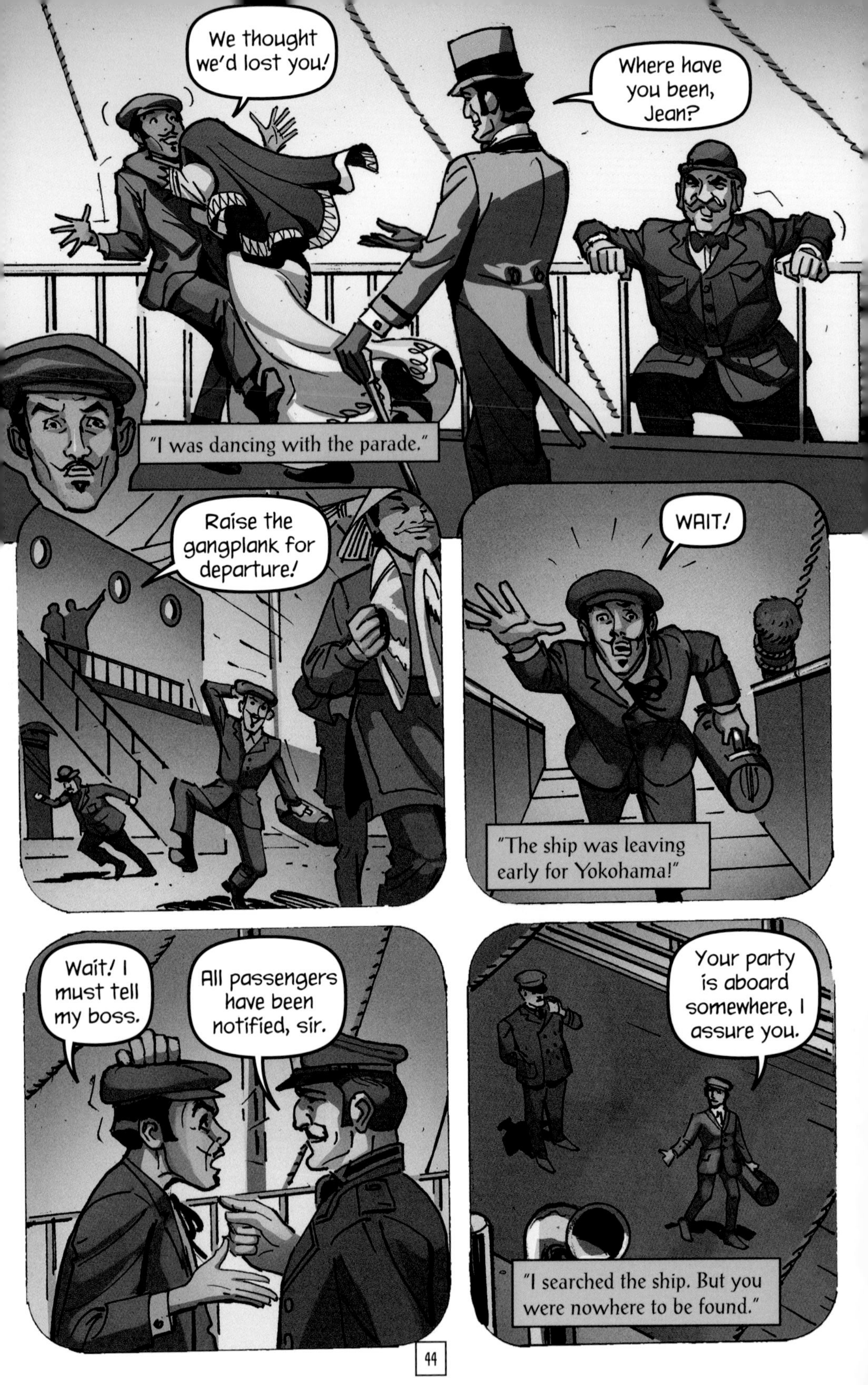

We thought we'd lost you!
Where have you been, Jean?
"I was dancing with the parade."
Raise the gangplank for departure!
WAIT!
"The ship was leaving early for Yokohama!"
Wait! I must tell my boss.
All passengers have been notified, sir.
Your party is aboard somewhere, I assure you.
"I searched the ship. But you were nowhere to be found."

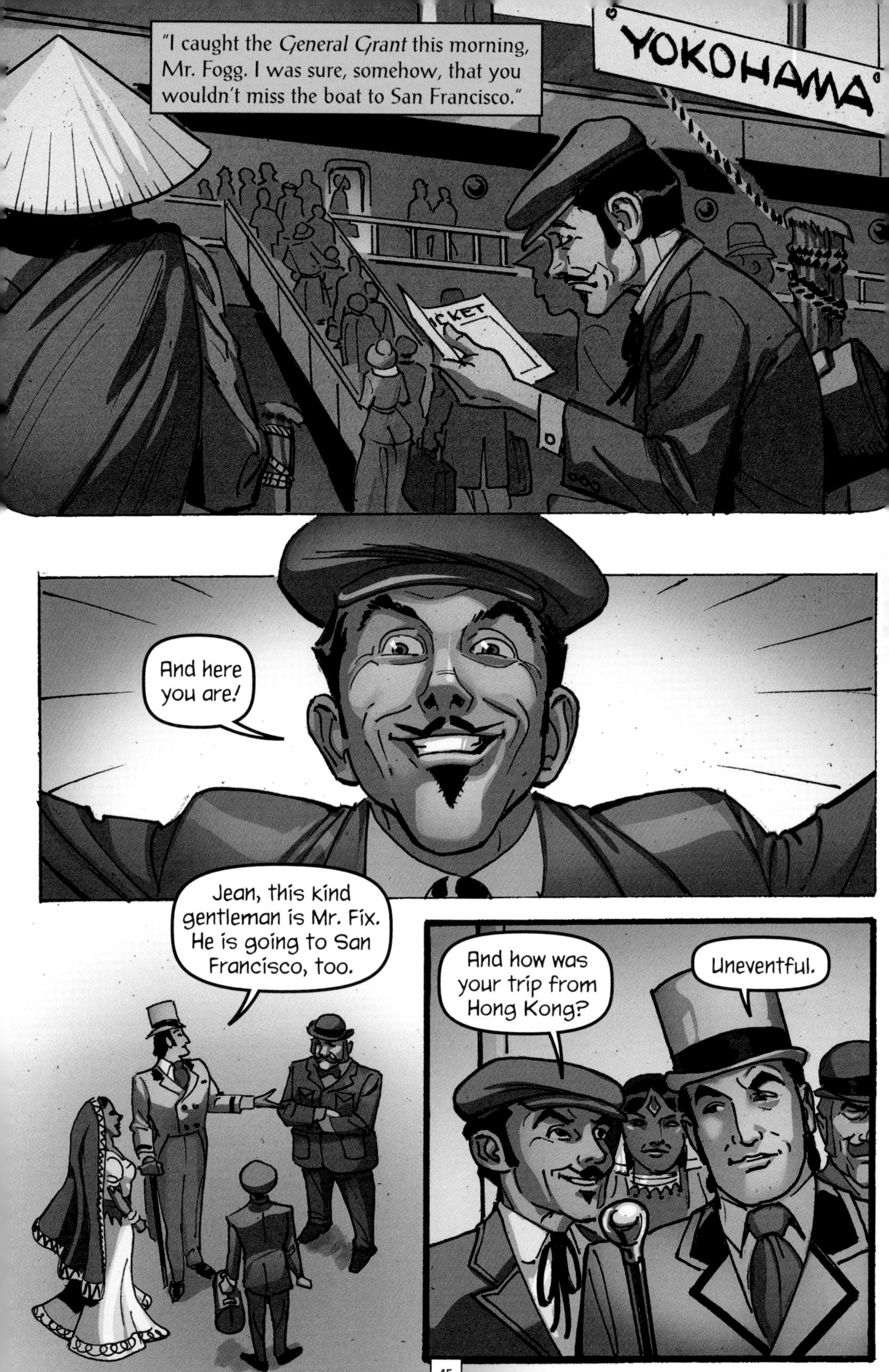
"I caught the *General Grant* this morning, Mr. Fogg. I was sure, somehow, that you wouldn't miss the boat to San Francisco."
YOKOHAMA
And here you are!
Jean, this kind gentleman is Mr. Fix. He is going to San Francisco, too.
And how was your trip from Hong Kong?
Uneventful.

CHAPTER 5
OBSTACLES

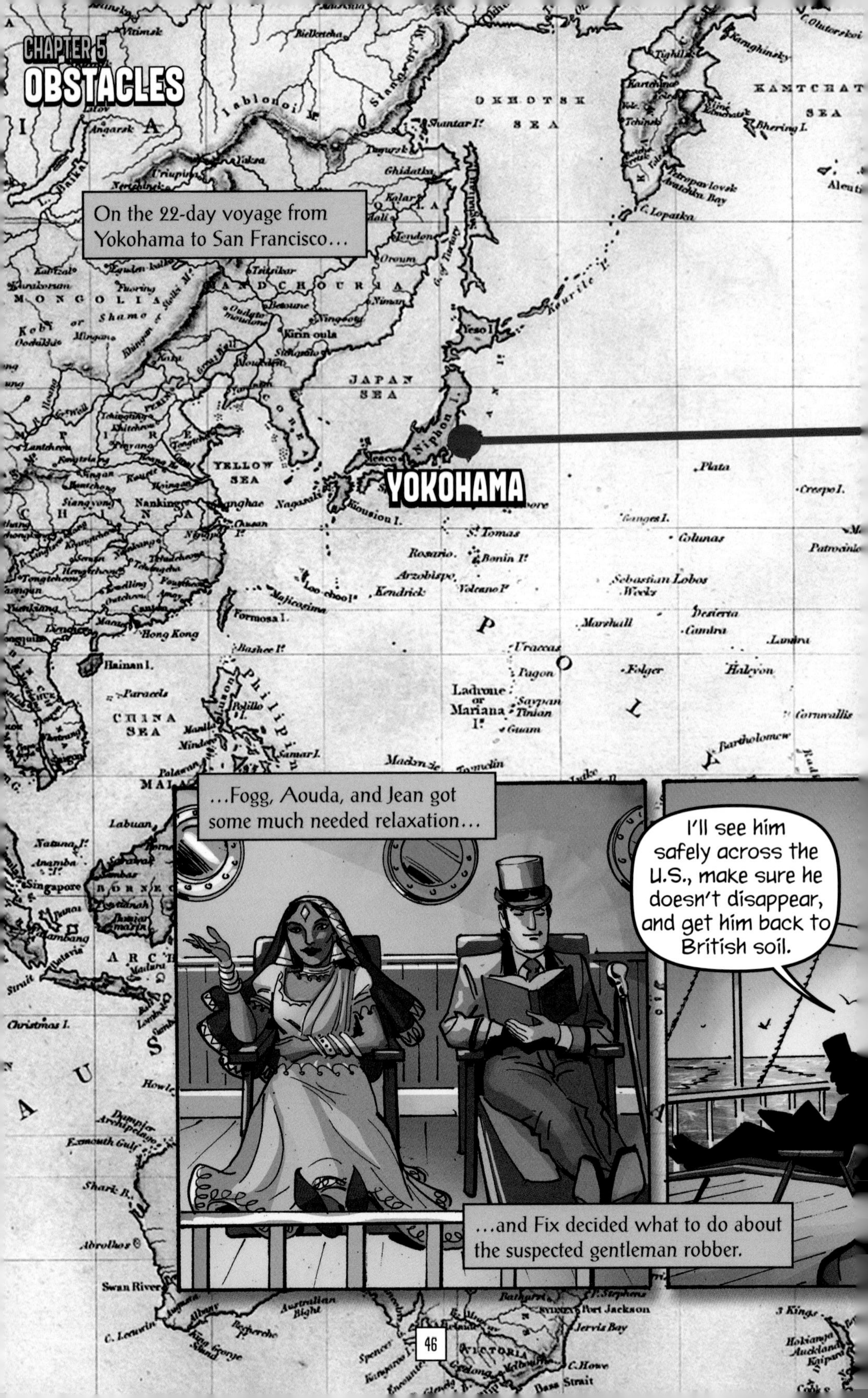

On the 22-day voyage from Yokohama to San Francisco...
YOKOHAMA
...Fogg, Aouda, and Jean got some much needed relaxation...
...and Fix decided what to do about the suspected gentleman robber.
I'll see him safely across the U.S., make sure he doesn't disappear, and get him back to British soil.

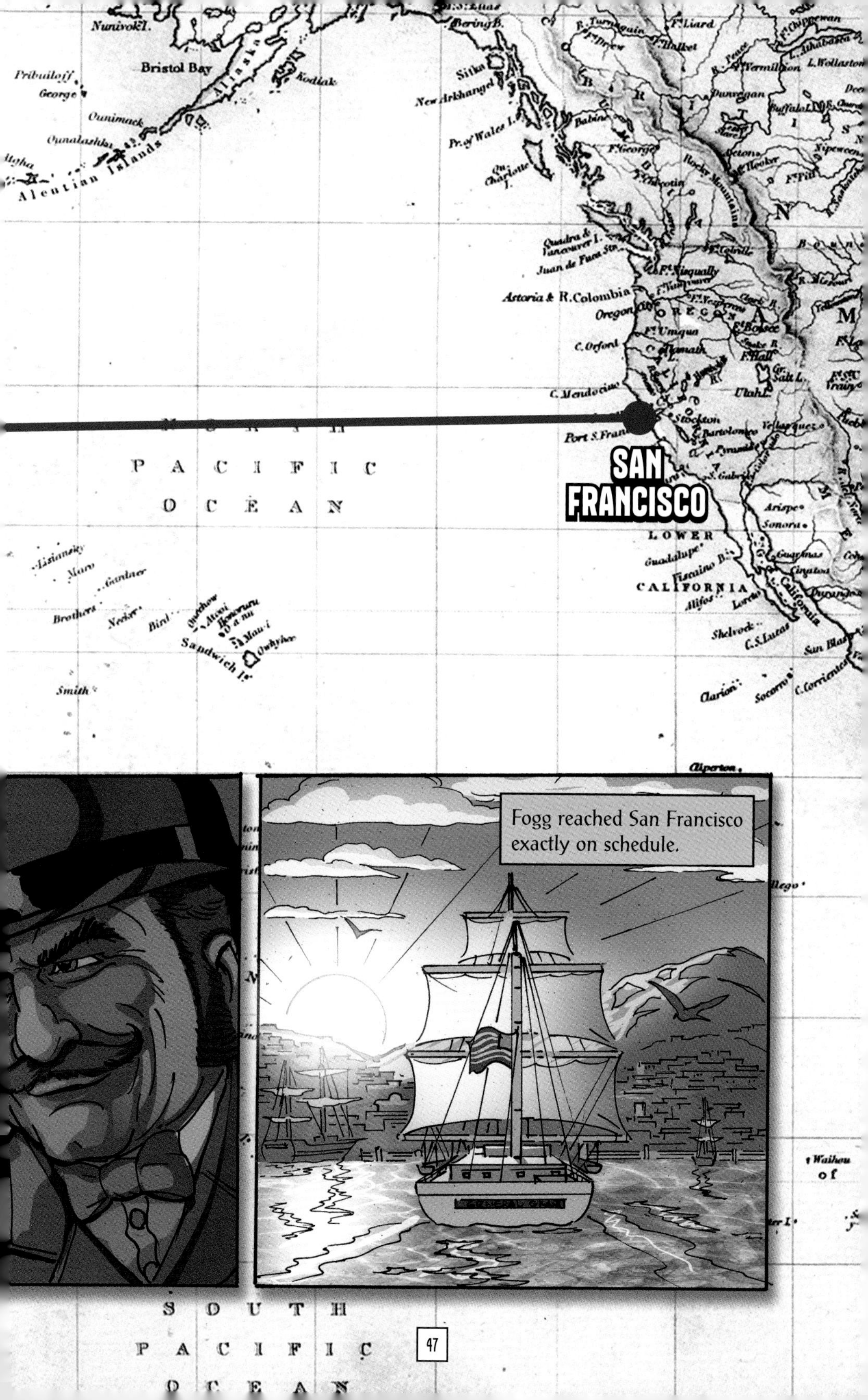
Nunivok I.
Bristol Bay
Aliaska
Kodiak
Pribuiloff
George
Ounimack
Ounalashka
Aleutian Islands
Sitka
New Arkhangel
Pr. of Wales I.
Qu. Charlotte I.
Rocky Mountains
Quadra & Vancouver I.
Juan de Fuca Str.
Astoria & R. Colombia
Oregon City
OREGON
C. Orford
C. Mendocino
Port S. Fran
Stockton
SAN FRANCISCO
PACIFIC
OCEAN
LOWER
CALIFORNIA
Guadalupe
Lisiansky
Maro
Gardner
Brothers
Necker
Bird
Sandwich I.
Owhyhee
Smith
Clarion
Socorro
C. Corrientes
San Blas
Clipperton
Fogg reached San Francisco exactly on schedule.
SOUTH
PACIFIC
OCEAN

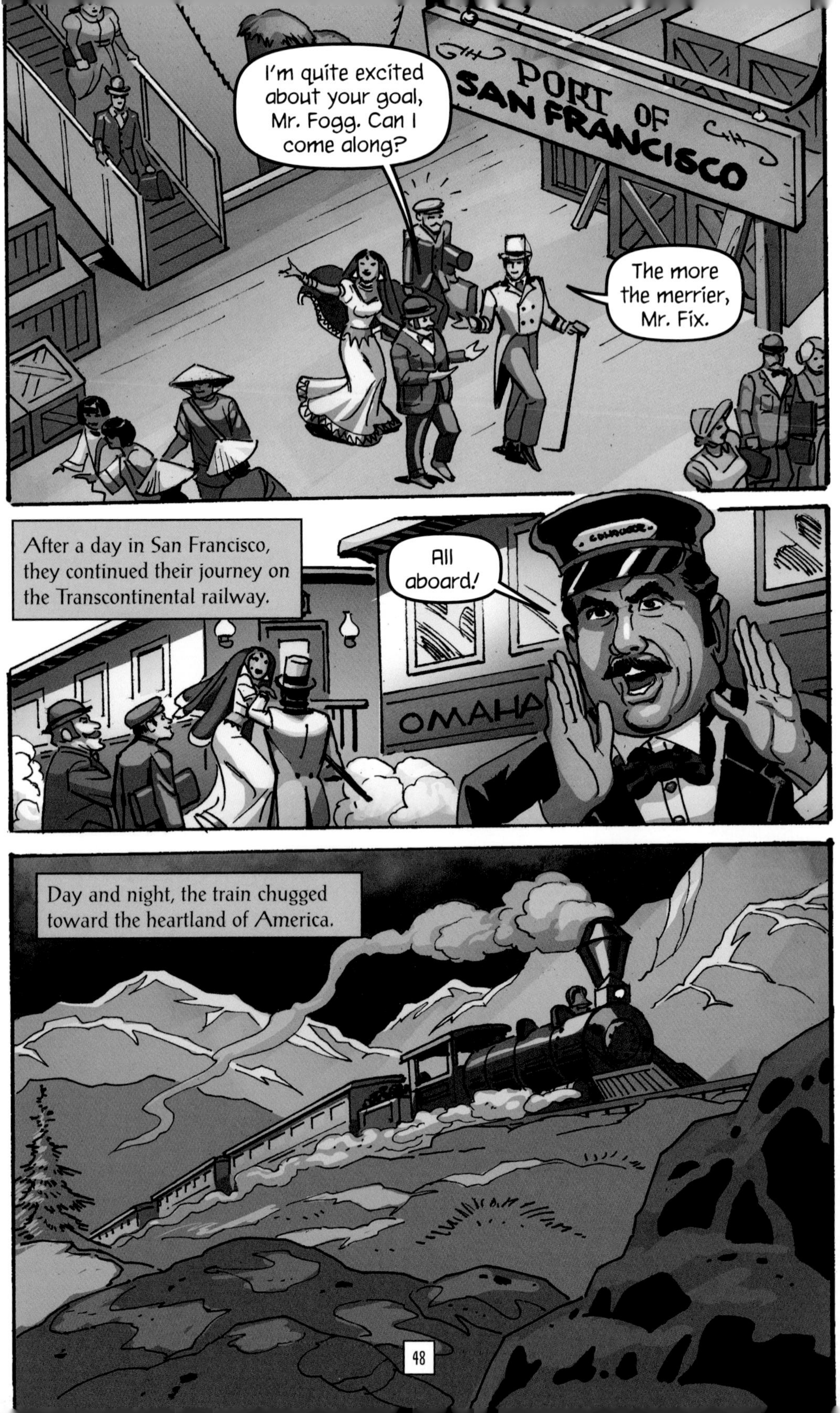

PORT OF SAN FRANCISCO
I'm quite excited about your goal, Mr. Fogg. Can I come along?
The more the merrier, Mr. Fix.
After a day in San Francisco, they continued their journey on the Transcontinental railway.
All aboard!
OMAHA
Day and night, the train chugged toward the heartland of America.

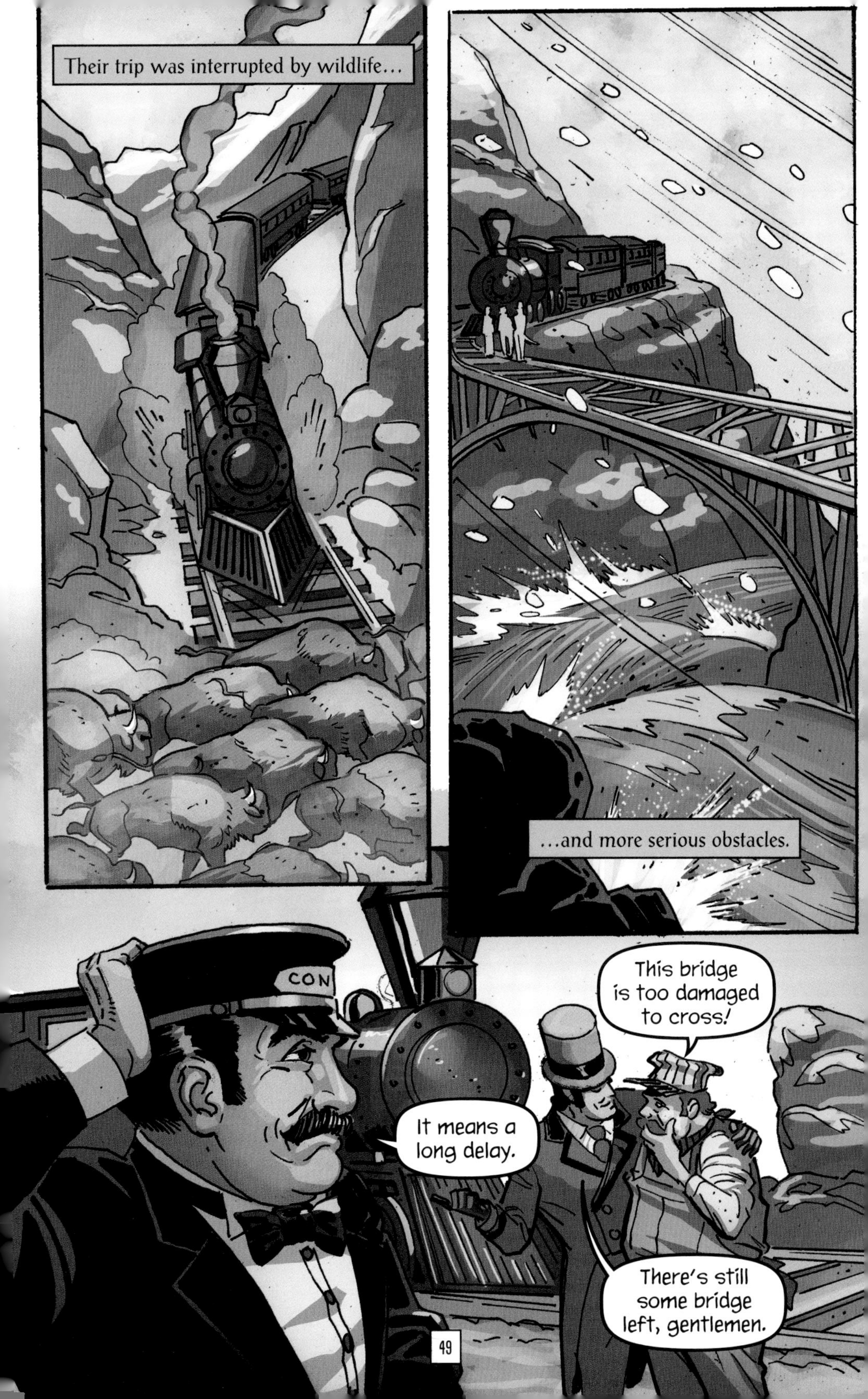
Their trip was interrupted by wildlife...
...and more serious obstacles.
CON
This bridge is too damaged to cross!
It means a long delay.
There's still some bridge left, gentlemen.

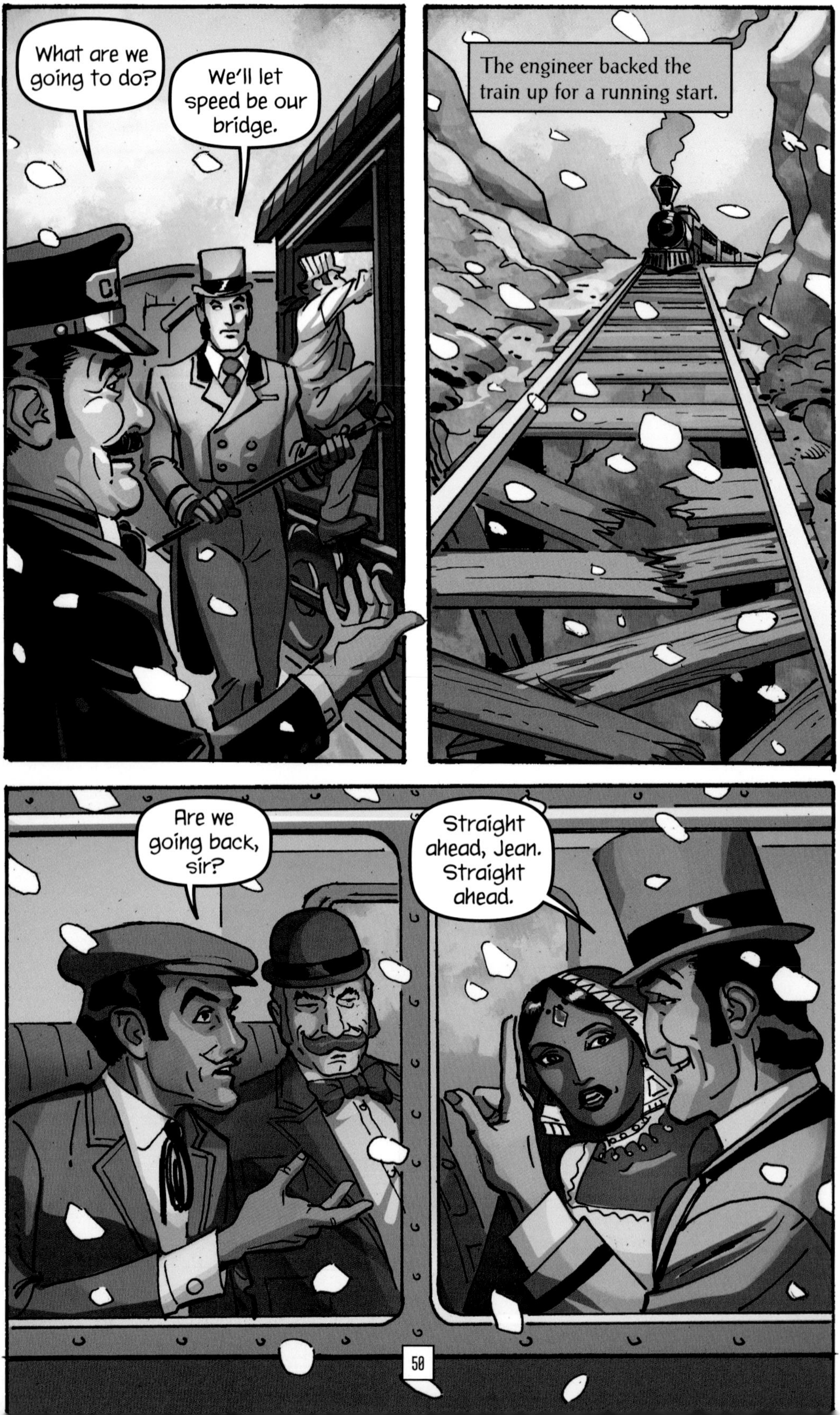
What are we going to do?
We'll let speed be our bridge.
The engineer backed the train up for a running start.
Are we going back, sir?
Straight ahead, Jean. Straight ahead.

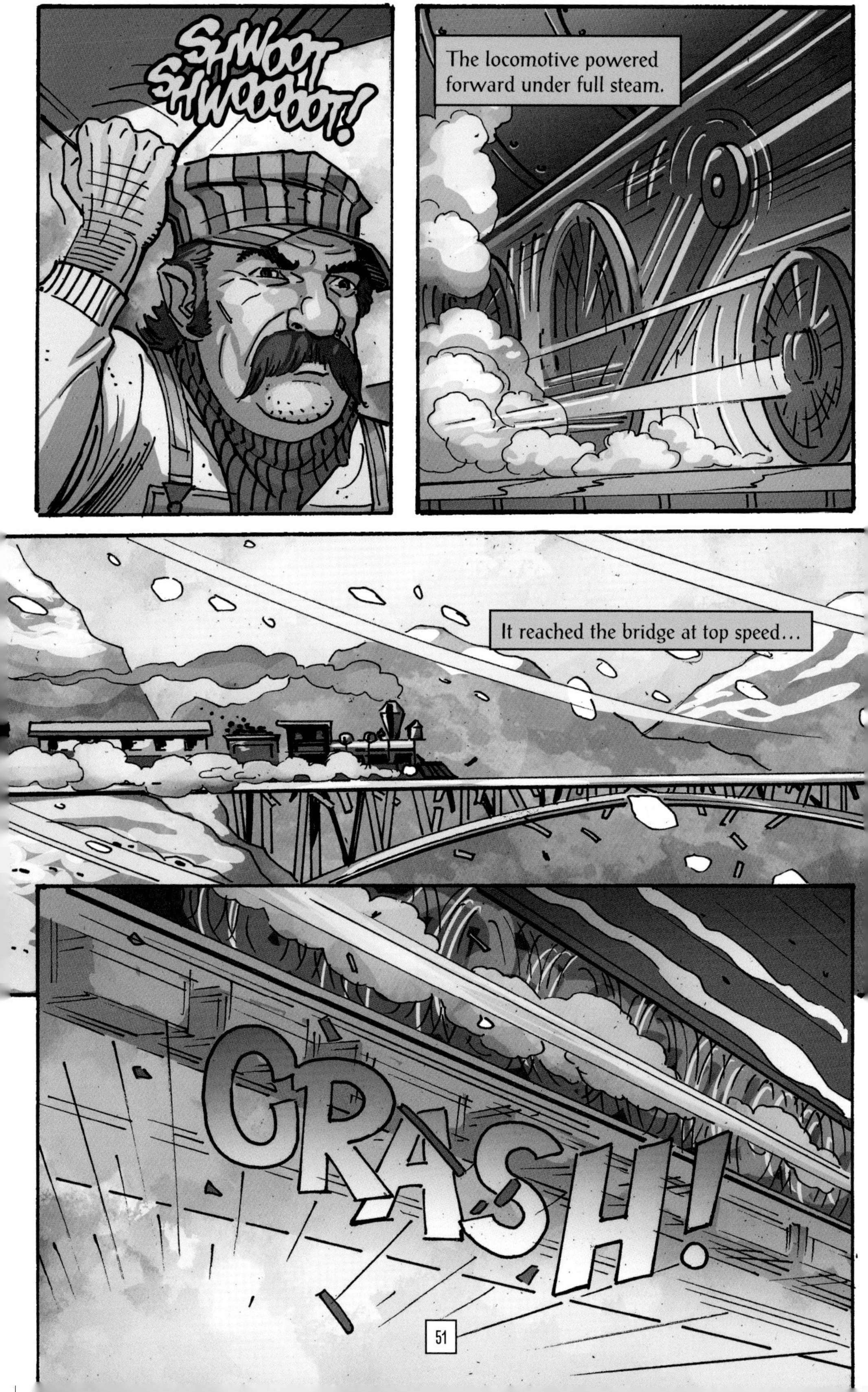
SHWOOT SHWOOOOOT!
The locomotive powered forward under full steam.
It reached the bridge at top speed...
CRASH!

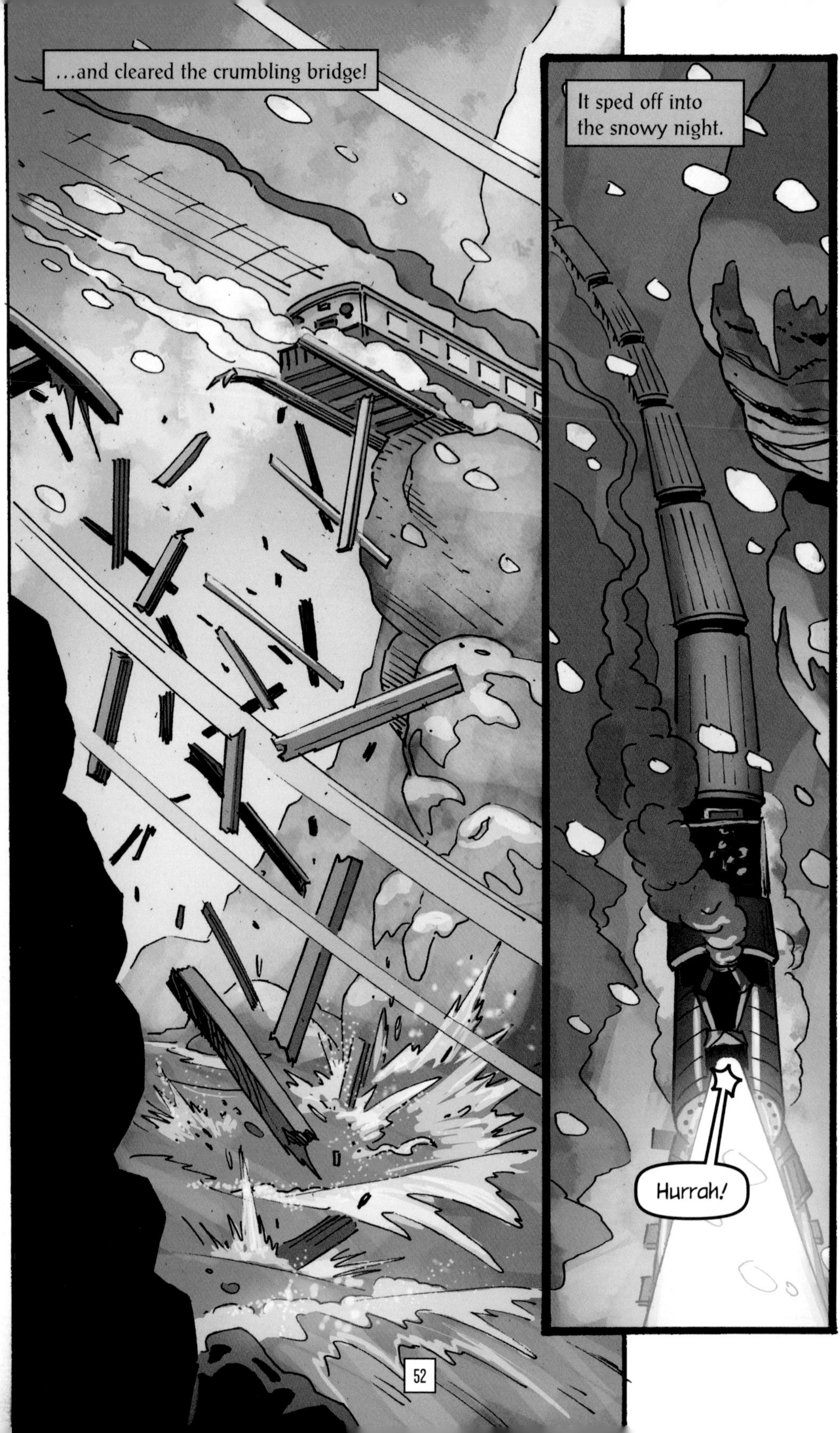
...and cleared the crumbling bridge!
It sped off into the snowy night.
Hurrah!

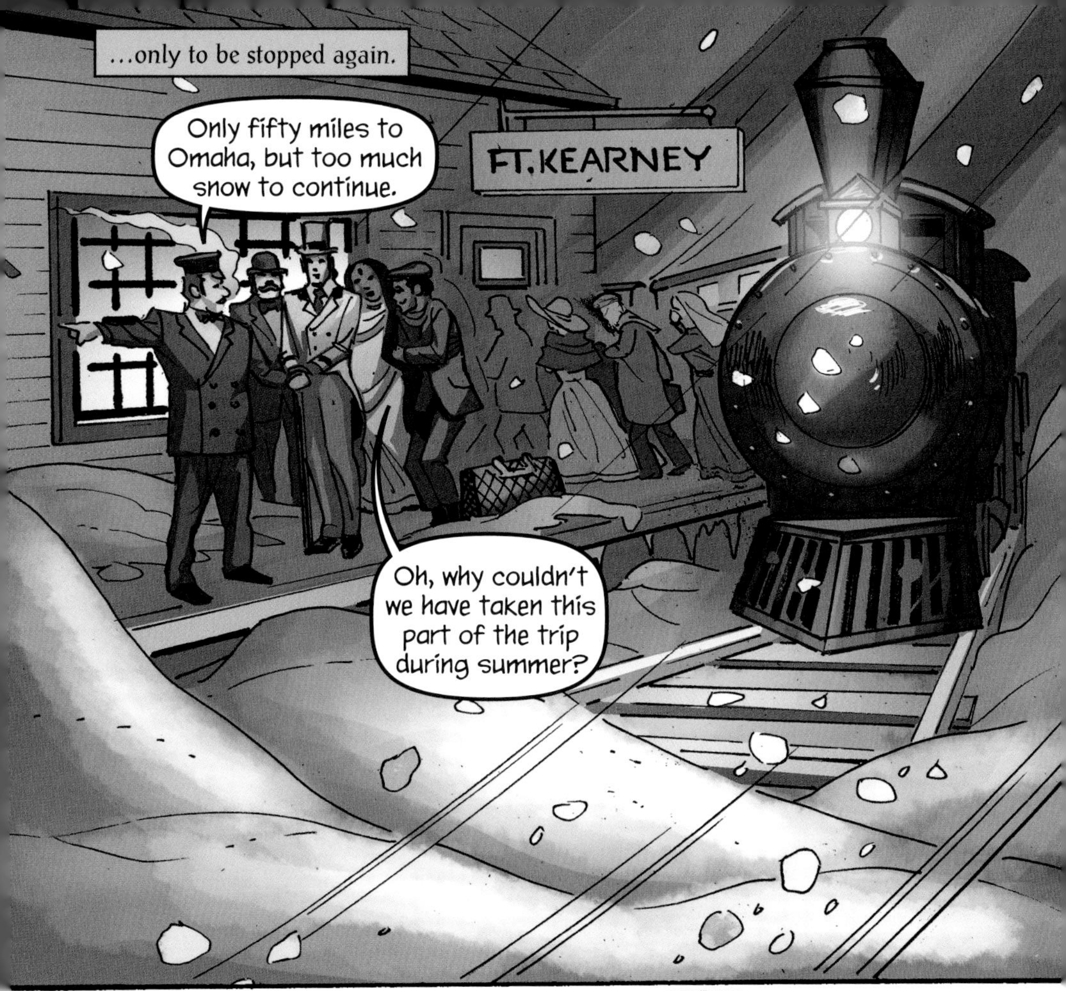
...only to be stopped again.
Only fifty miles to Omaha, but too much snow to continue.
FT. KEARNEY
Oh, why couldn't we have taken this part of the trip during summer?

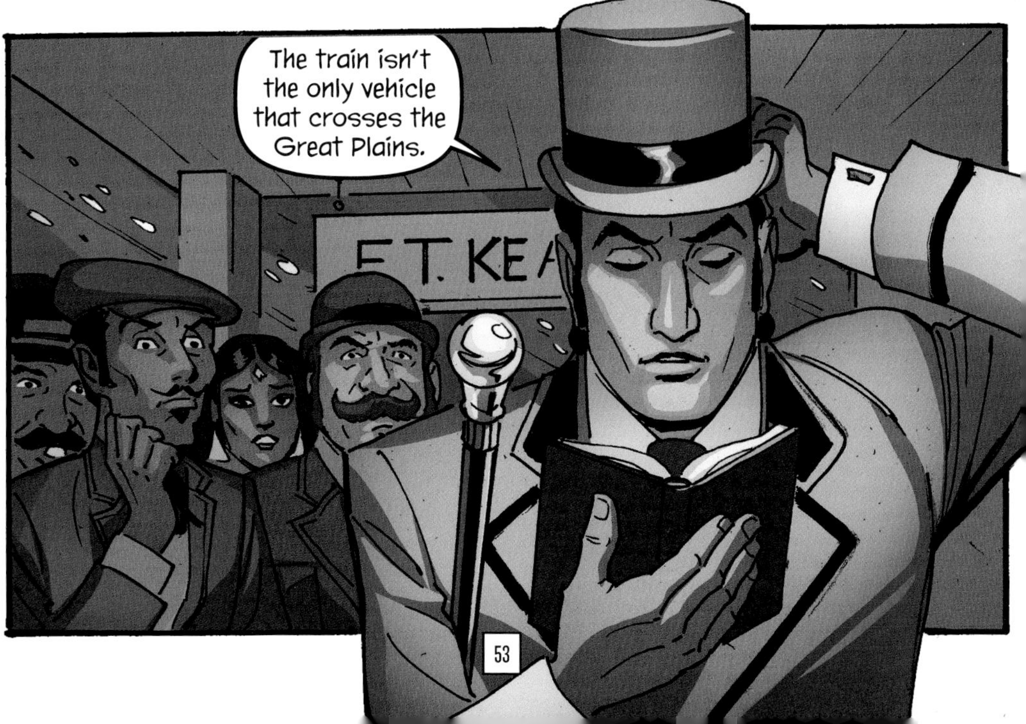
The train isn't the only vehicle that crosses the Great Plains.

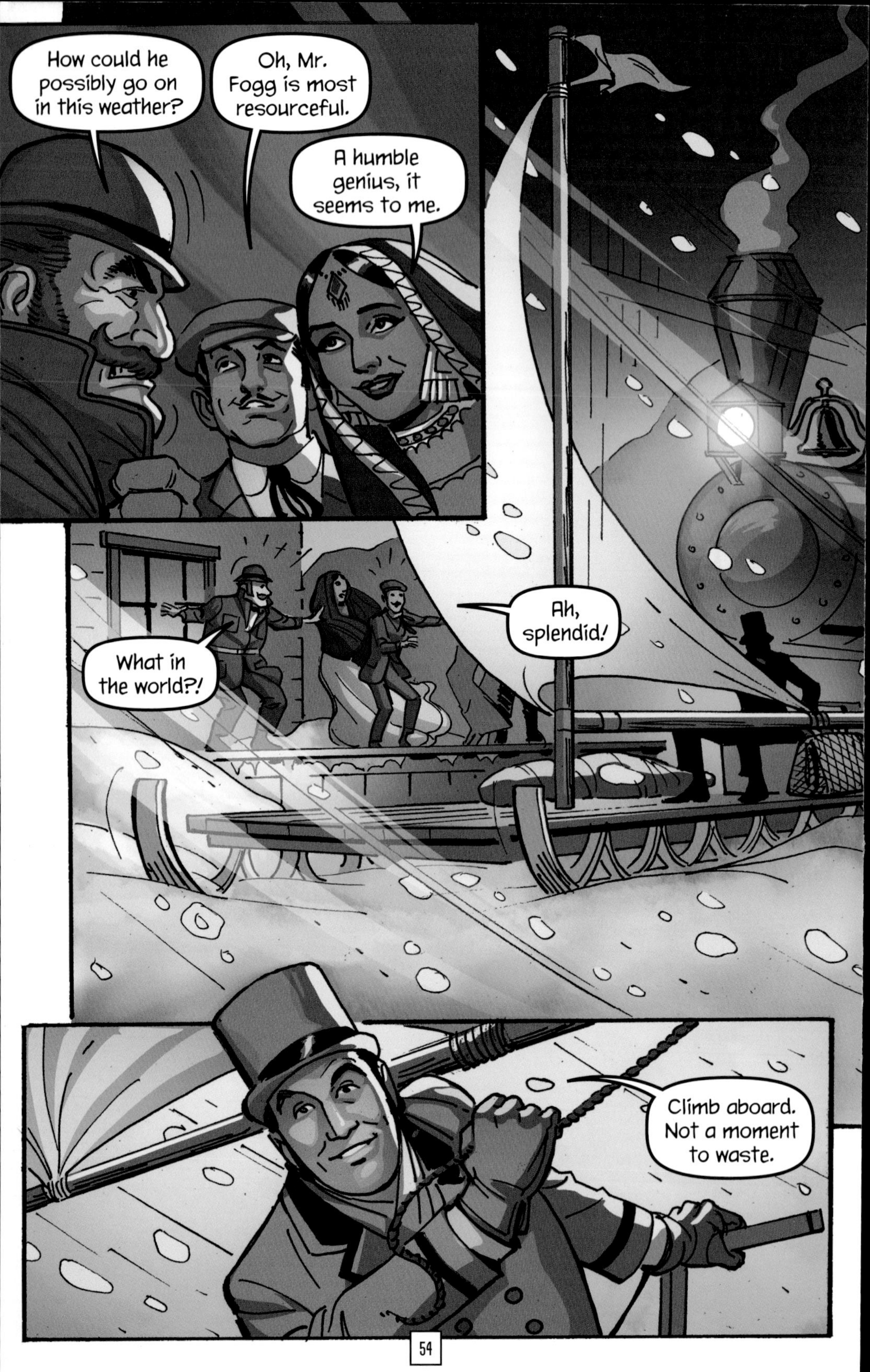
How could he possibly go on in this weather?
Oh, Mr. Fogg is most resourceful.
A humble genius, it seems to me.
What in the world?!
Ah, splendid!
Climb aboard. Not a moment to waste.

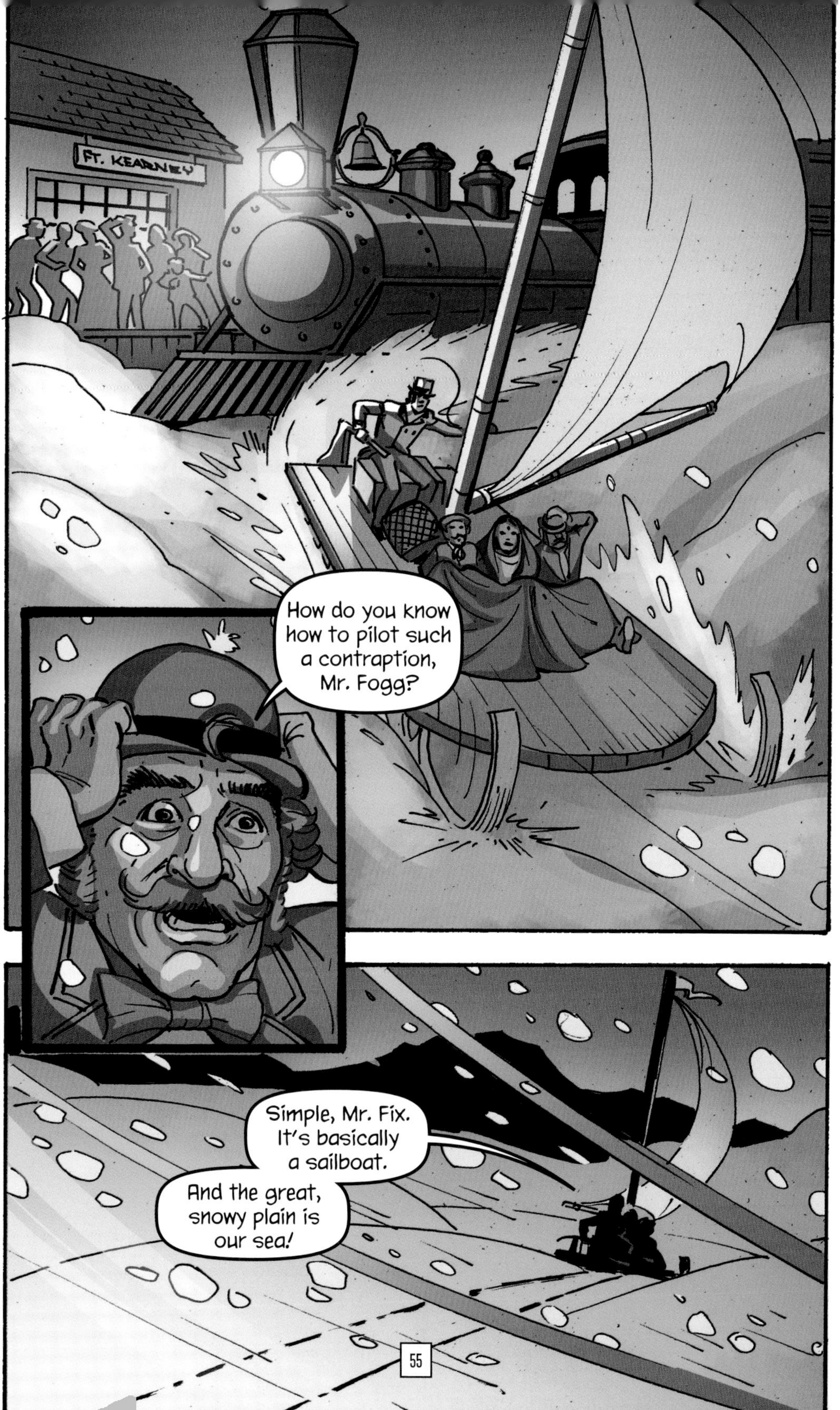
FT. KEARNEY
How do you know how to pilot such a contraption, Mr. Fogg?
Simple, Mr. Fix. It's basically a sailboat.
And the great, snowy plain is our sea!

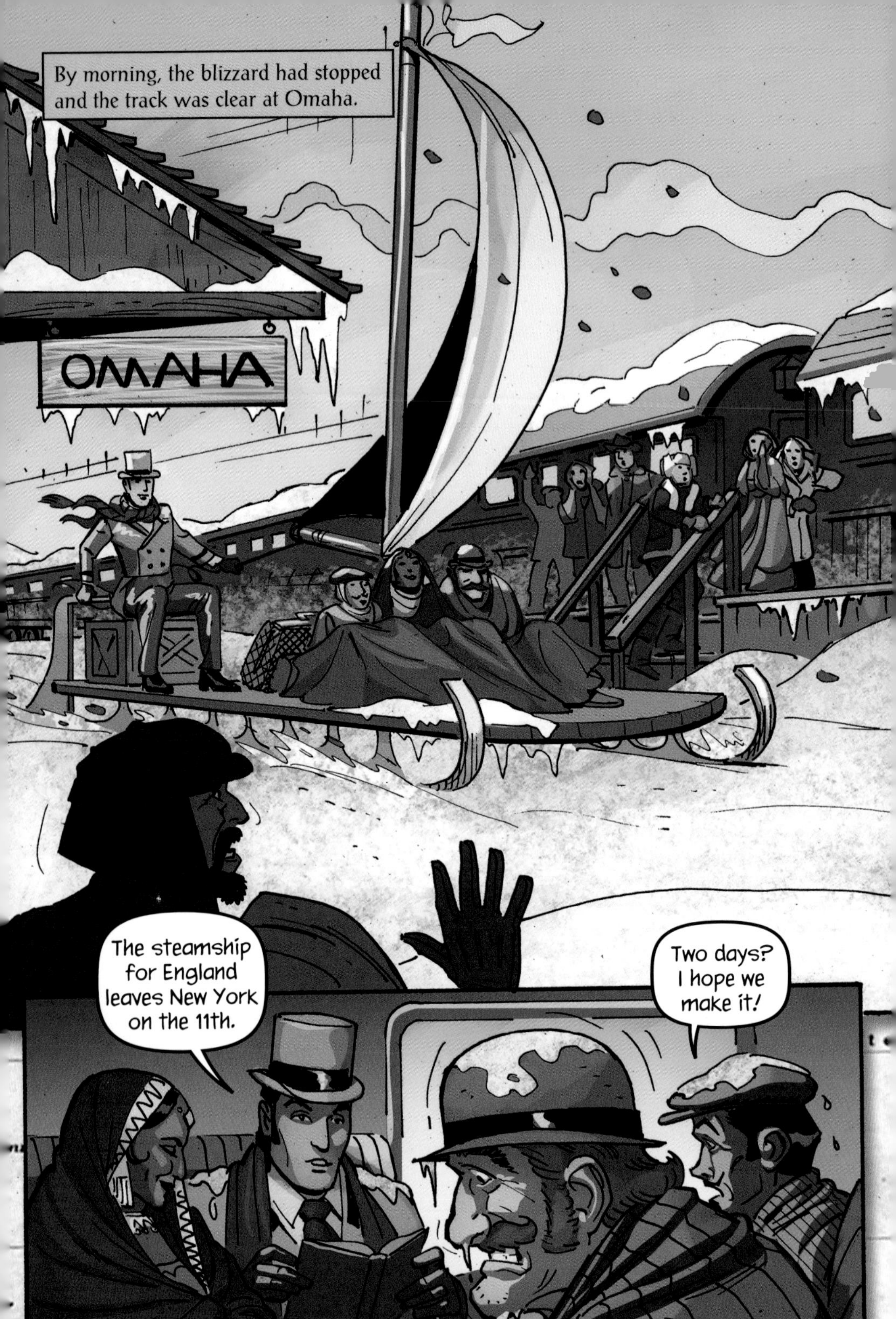
By morning, the blizzard had stopped and the track was clear at Omaha.
OMAHA
The steamship for England leaves New York on the 11th.
Two days? I hope we make it!

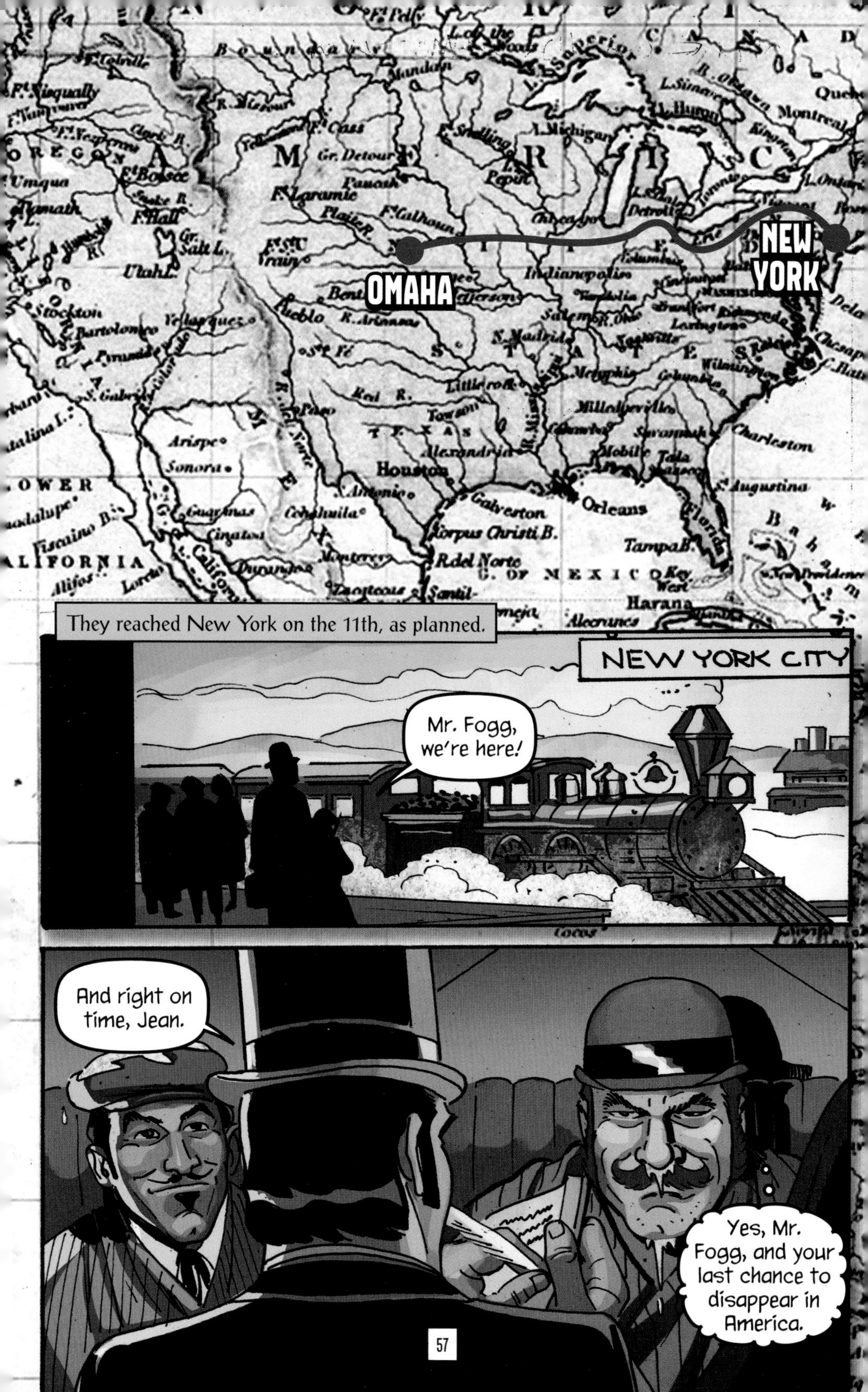
OMAHA
NEW YORK
They reached New York on the 11th, as planned.
NEW YORK CITY
Mr. Fogg, we're here!
And right on time, Jean.
Yes, Mr. Fogg, and your last chance to disappear in America.

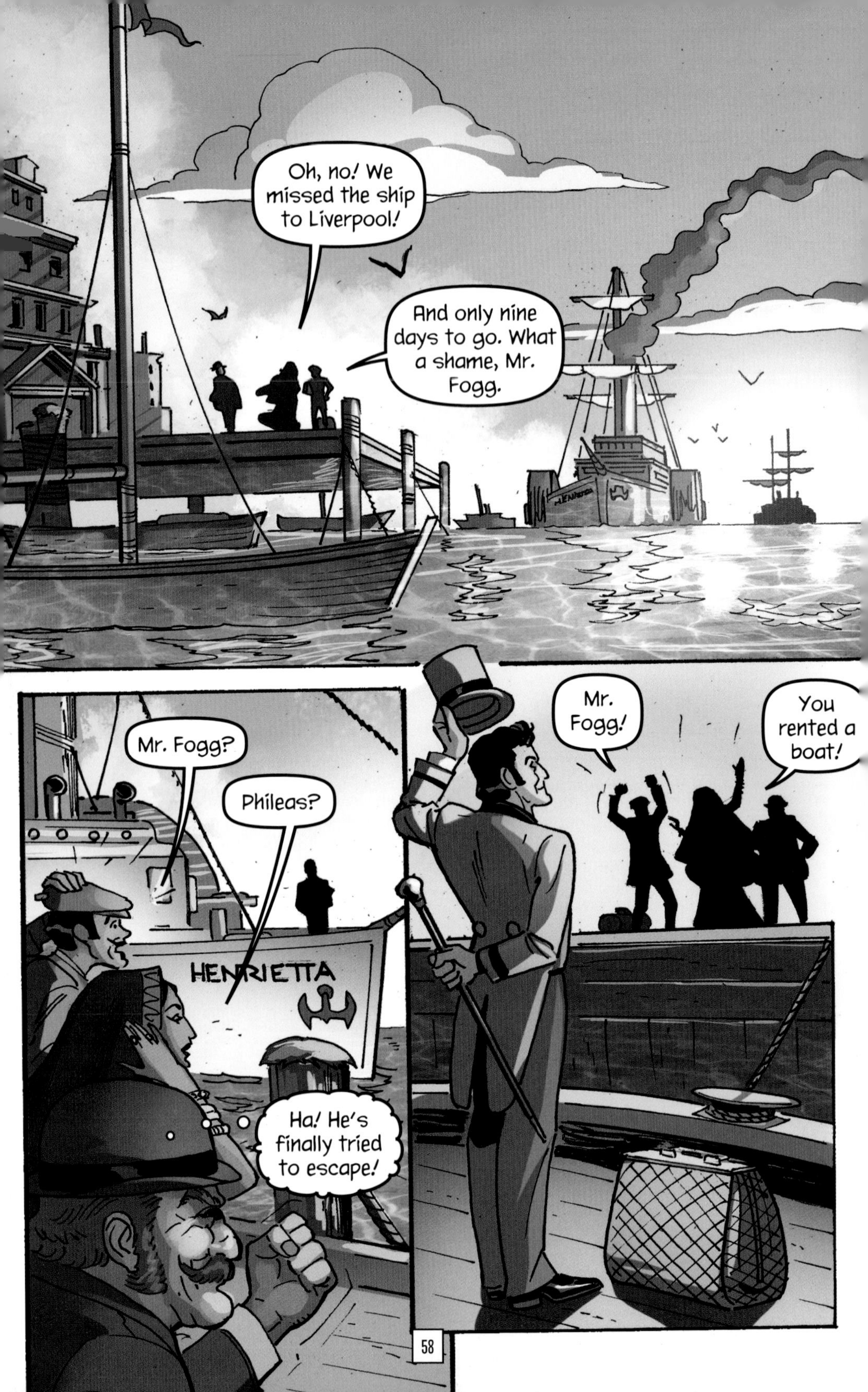
Oh, no! We missed the ship to Liverpool!
And only nine days to go. What a shame, Mr. Fogg.
HENRIETTA
Mr. Fogg?
Phileas?
Ha! He's finally tried to escape!
Mr. Fogg!
You rented a boat!

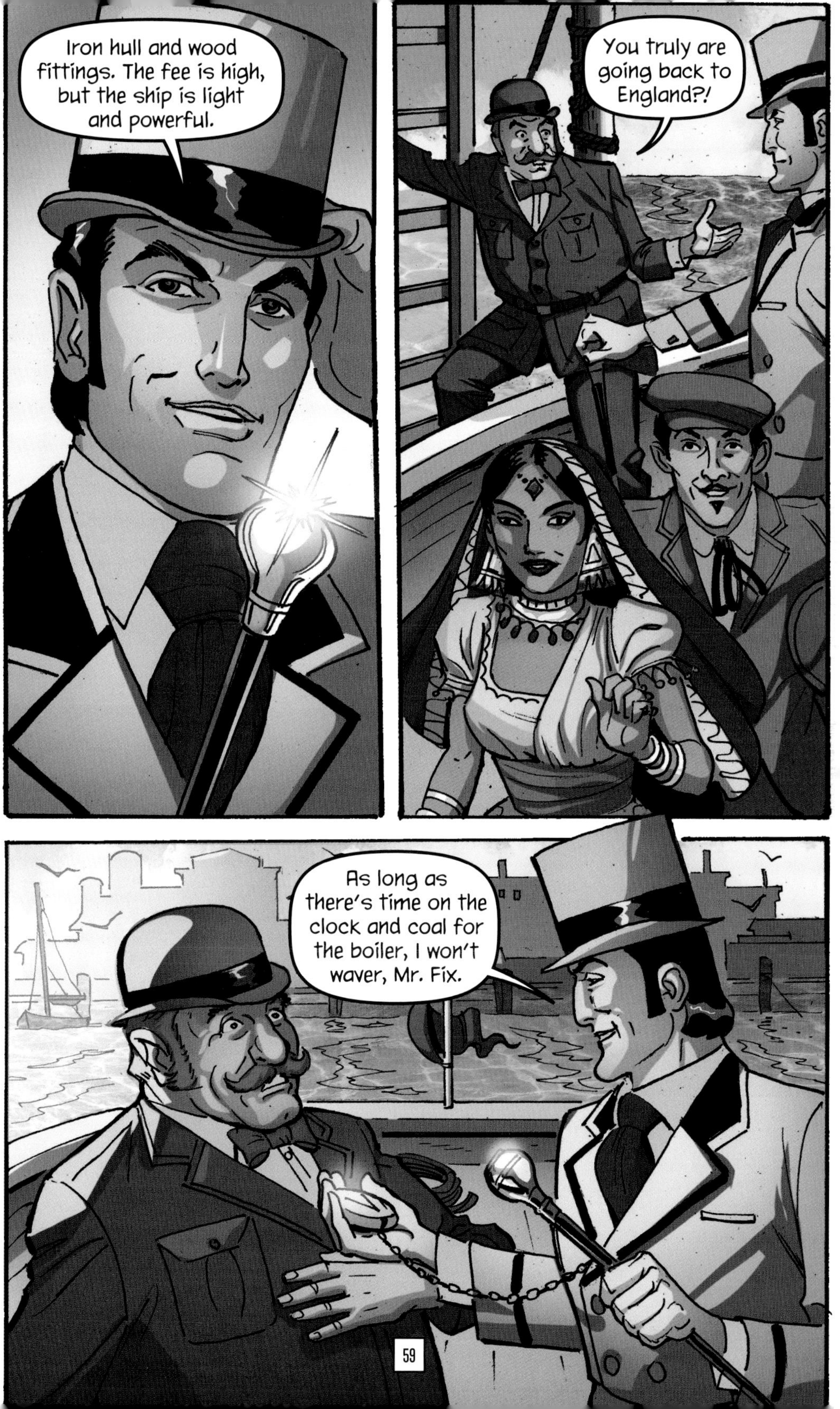
Iron hull and wood fittings. The fee is high, but the ship is light and powerful.
You truly are going back to England?!
As long as there's time on the clock and coal for the boiler, I won't waver, Mr. Fix.
59

CHAPTER 6
UNDERFOOT

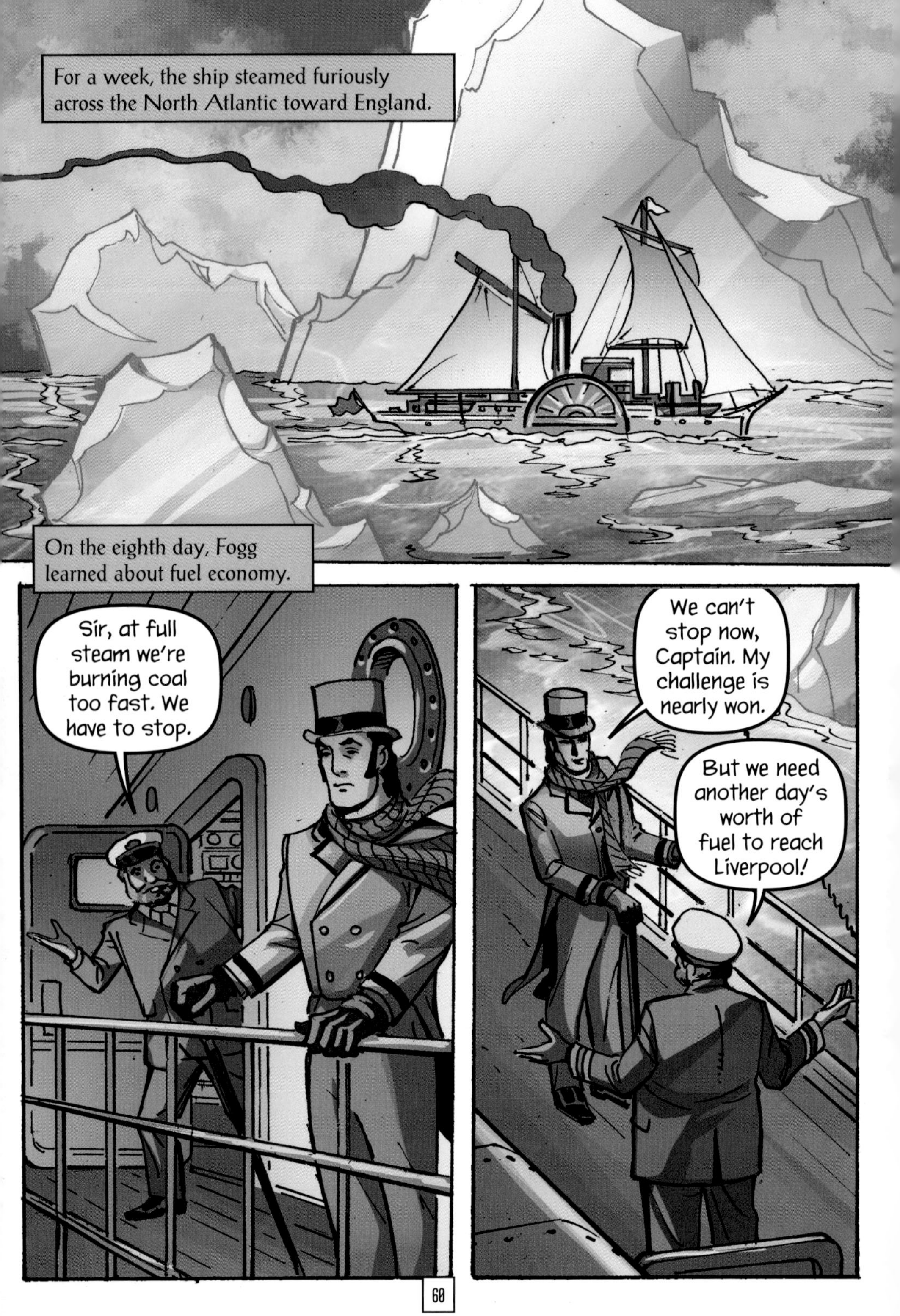
For a week, the ship steamed furiously across the North Atlantic toward England.
On the eighth day, Fogg learned about fuel economy.
Sir, at full steam we're burning coal too fast. We have to stop.
We can't stop now, Captain. My challenge is nearly won.
But we need another day's worth of fuel to reach Liverpool!

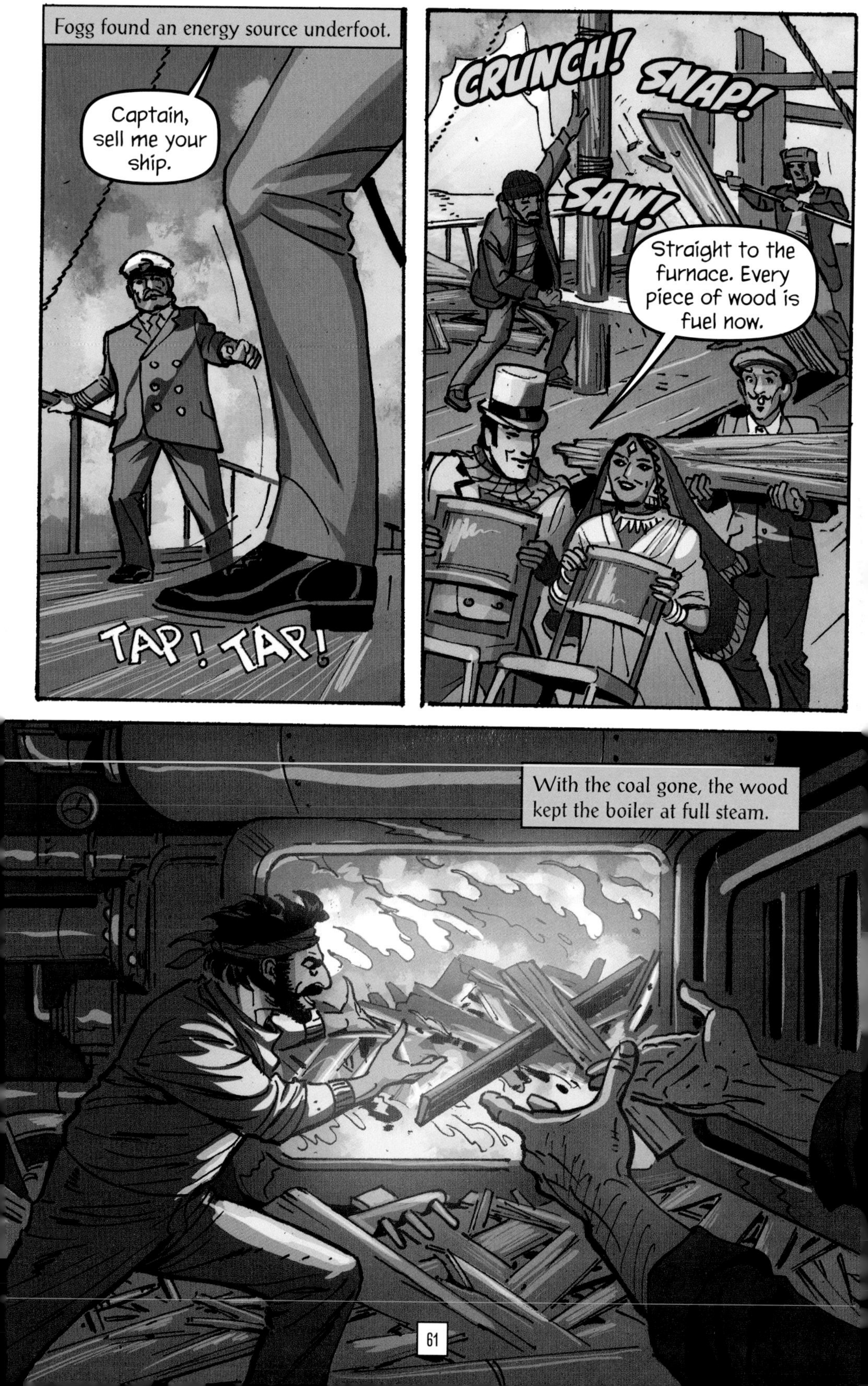
Fogg found an energy source underfoot.
Captain, sell me your ship.
TAP! TAP!
CRUNCH!
SNAP!
SAW!
Straight to the furnace. Every piece of wood is fuel now.
With the coal gone, the wood kept the boiler at full steam.

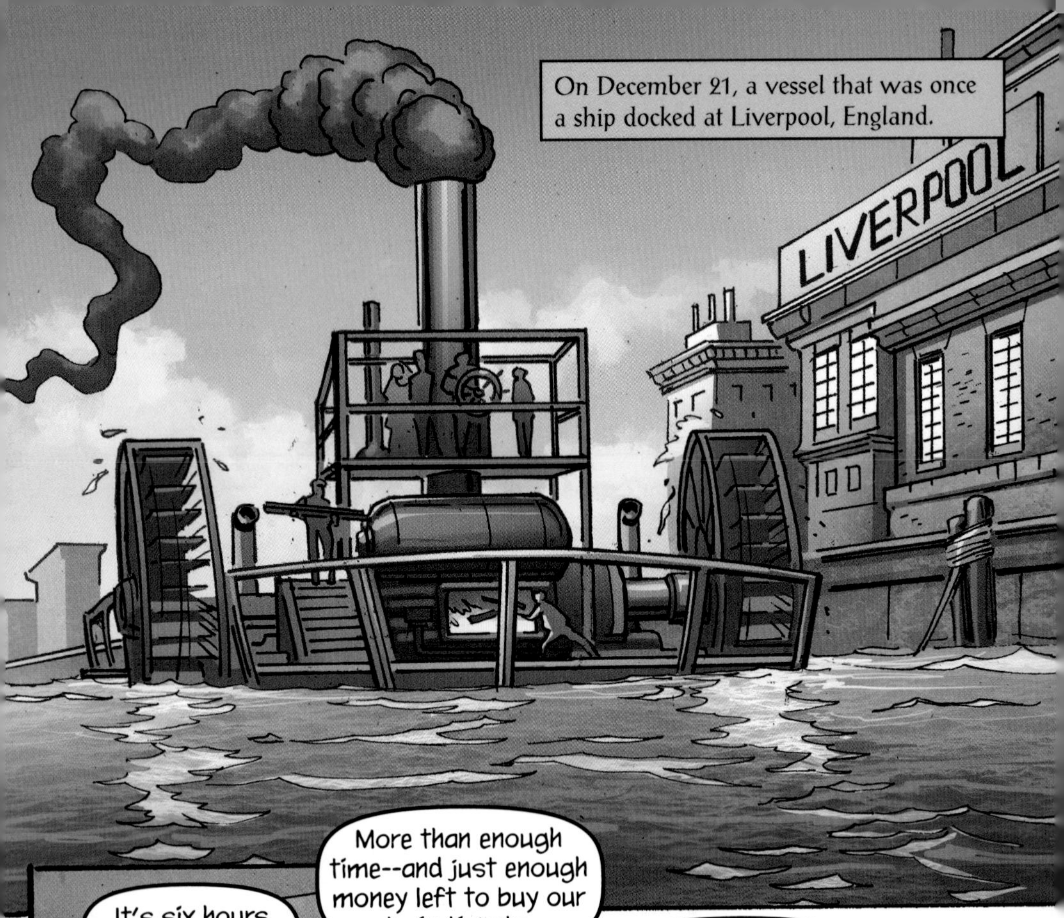
On December 21, a vessel that was once a ship docked at Liverpool, England.
LIVERPOOL

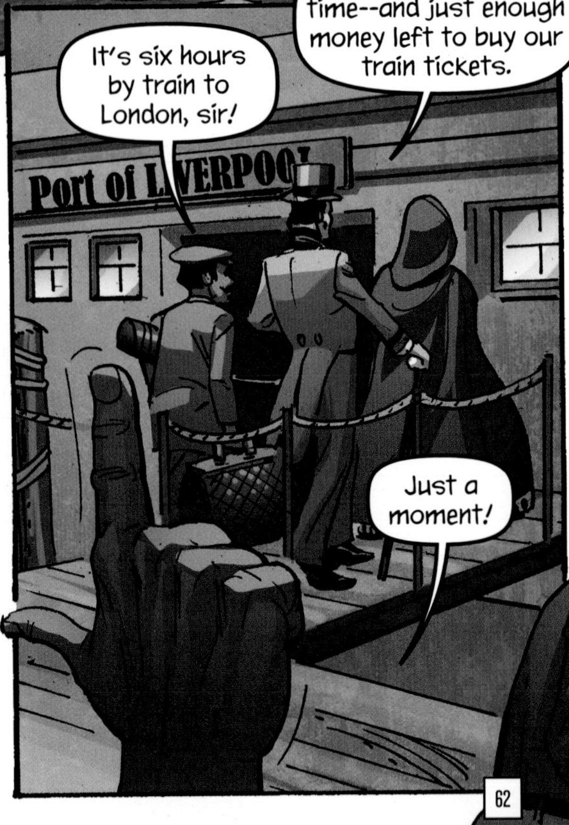
It's six hours by train to London, sir!
More than enough time--and just enough money left to buy our train tickets.
Port of LIVERPOOL
Just a moment!

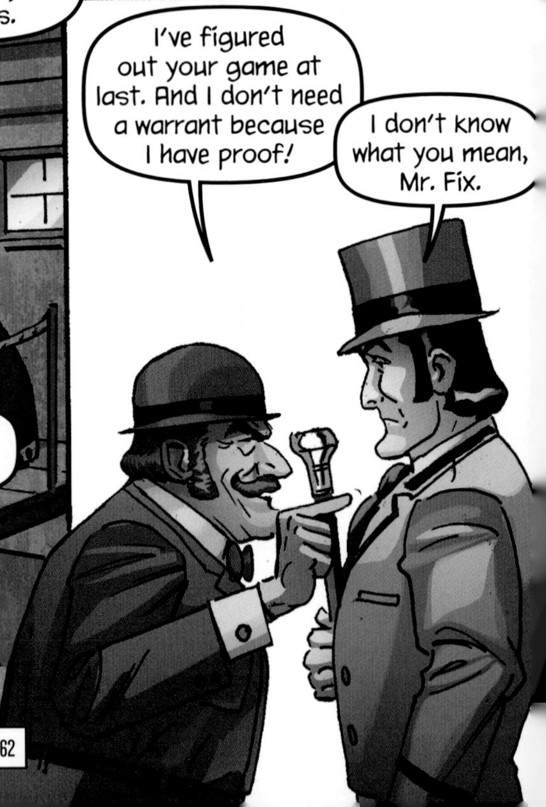
I've figured out your game at last. And I don't need a warrant because I have proof!
I don't know what you mean, Mr. Fix.

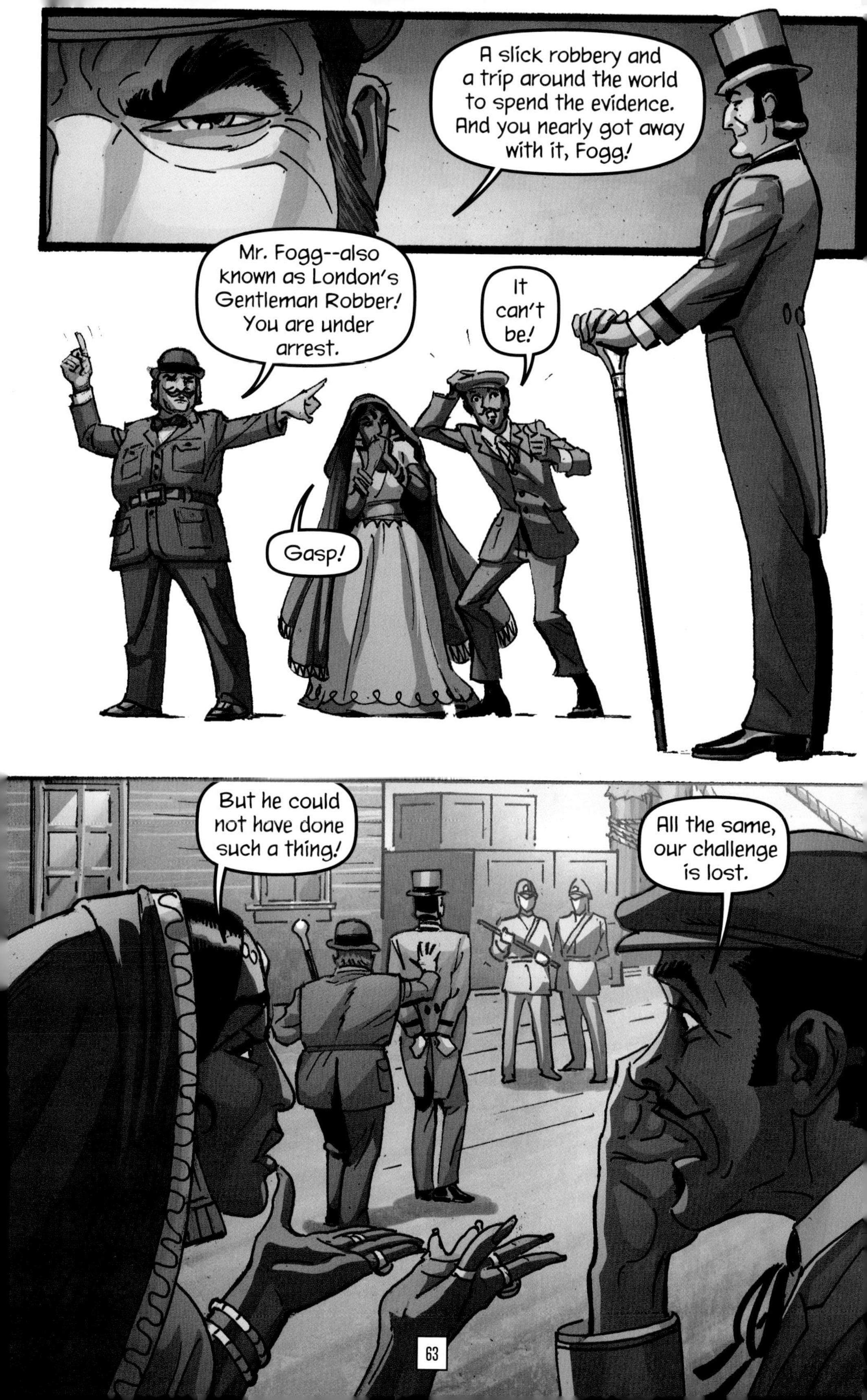
A slick robbery and a trip around the world to spend the evidence. And you nearly got away with it, Fogg!
Mr. Fogg--also known as London's Gentleman Robber! You are under arrest.
It can't be!
Gasp!
But he could not have done such a thing!
All the same, our challenge is lost.

CHAPTER 7
80 DAYS

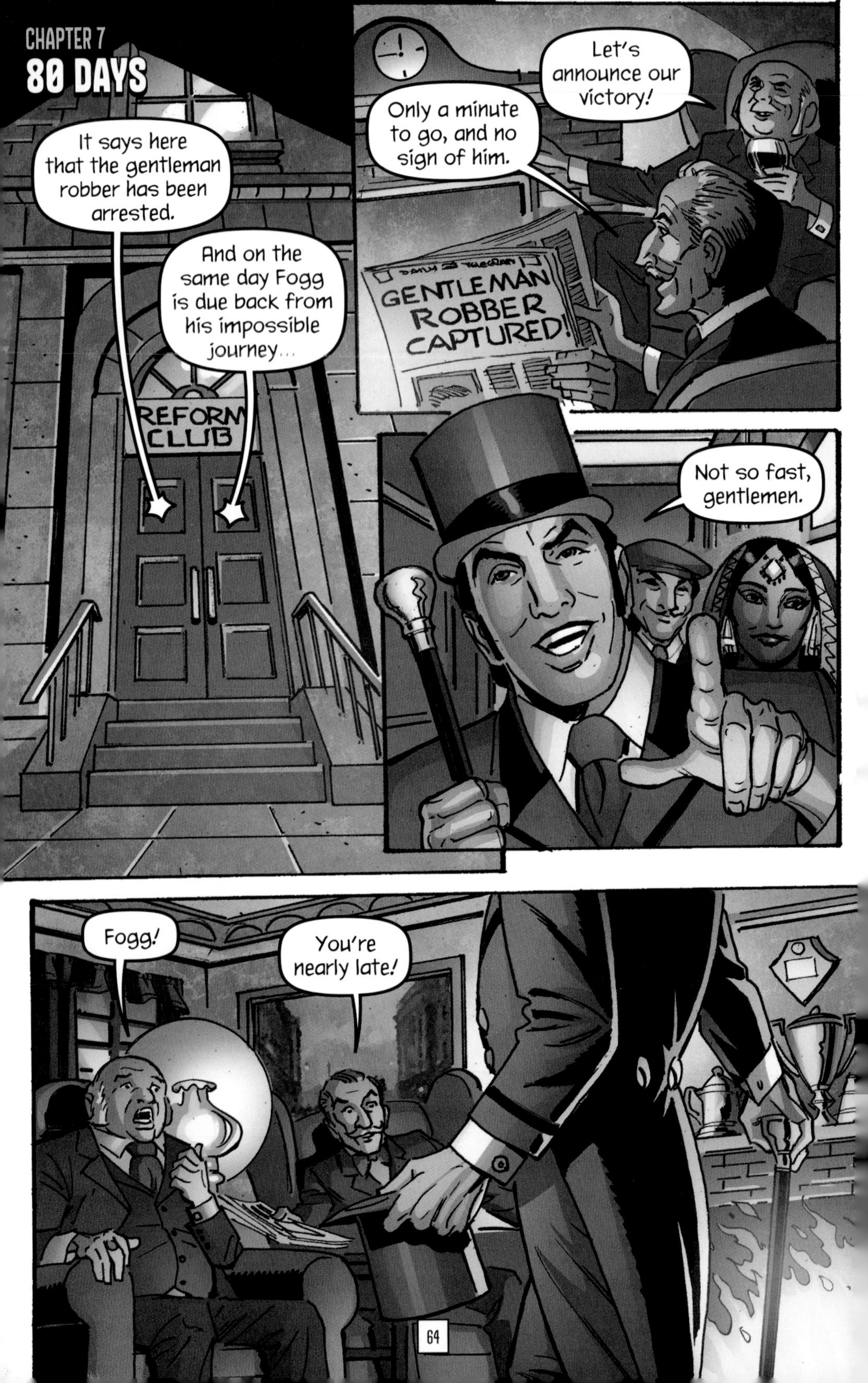

It says here that the gentleman robber has been arrested.
And on the same day Fogg is due back from his impossible journey...
REFORM CLUB
Only a minute to go, and no sign of him.
Let's announce our victory!
GENTLEMAN ROBBER CAPTURED!
Not so fast, gentlemen.
Fogg!
You're nearly late!

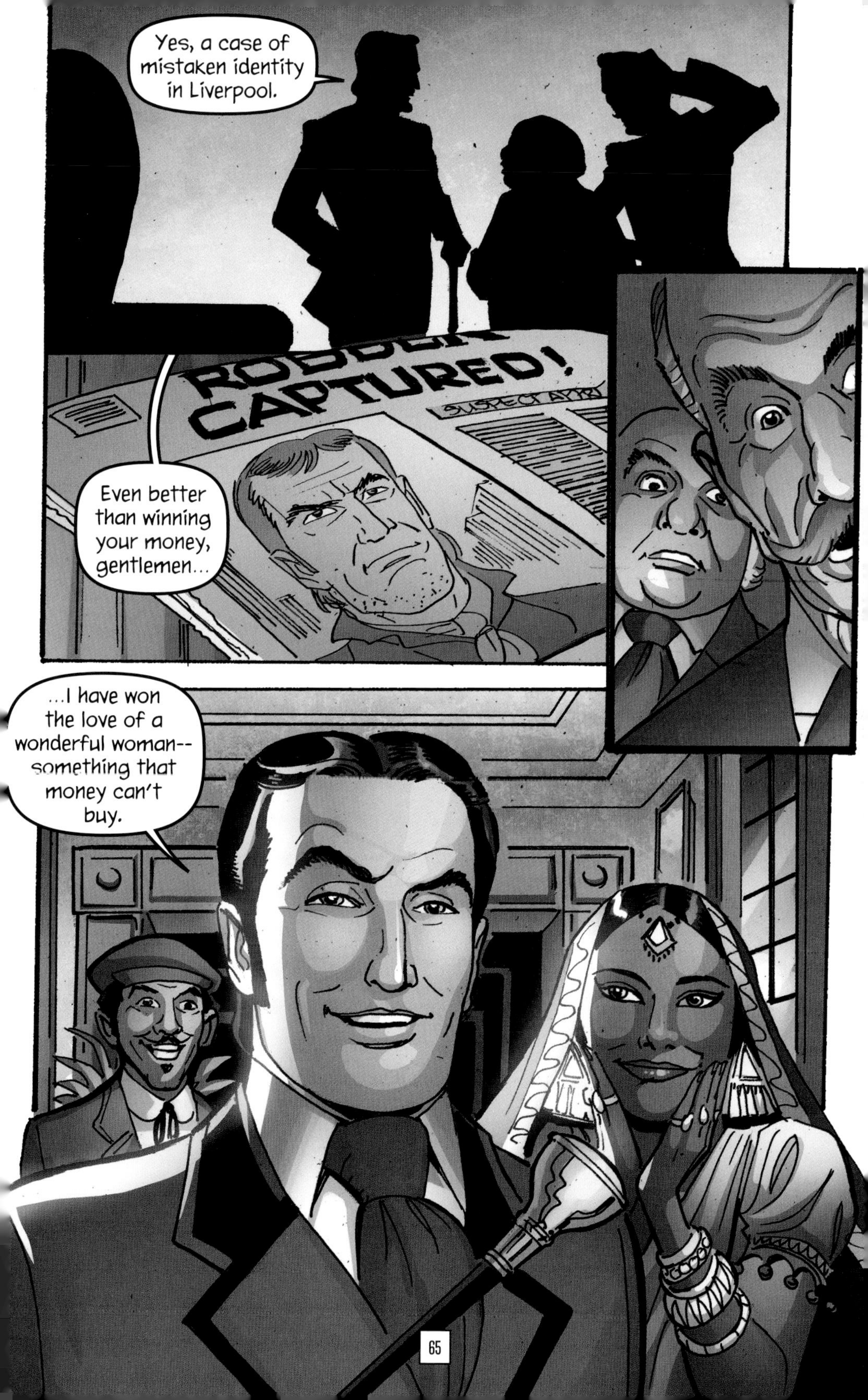
Yes, a case of mistaken identity in Liverpool.
CAPTURED!
Even better than winning your money, gentlemen...
...I have won the love of a wonderful woman--something that money can't buy.

ABOUT THE RETELLING AUTHOR AND ILLUSTRATOR

Chris Everheart always dreamed of interesting places, fascinating people, and exciting adventures. He is still a dreamer. He enjoys writing thrilling stories about young heroes who live in a world that doesn't always understand them. Chris lives in Minneapolis, Minnesota with his family. He plans to travel to every continent on the globe, see interesting places, meet fascinating people, and have exciting adventures — much like Phileas Fogg and his travel mates!

Tod Smith is a self-employed illustrator and a graduate of the Joe Kubert School of Cartooning and Graphic Art. He has illustrated a wide variety of books, including work for companies like Marvel. He currently lives in Hartford, Connecticut.

GLOSSARY

arrest (uh-RESST)—to use the power of the law to take and keep someone in custody

boiler (BOY-ler)—a large container in which water is heated to produce steam in an engine

piston (PISS-tuhn)—a part of an engine that moves up and down inside a tube, causing other parts of the engine to move

propeller (pruh-PELL-er)—a device with two or more blades that turn quickly and cause a ship or aircraft to move

rajah (RAH-juh)—a king or prince in India

ritual (RI-choo-uhl)—a formal ceremony or series of acts that is always performed in the same way

sacrifice (SAK-ri-fahyss)—an act of killing a person or animal in a religious ceremony to please a god

tame (TAYM)—not wild, or trained to obey people

warrant (WAHR-uhnt)—a document issued by a court that gives the police the power to do something, like arrest someone

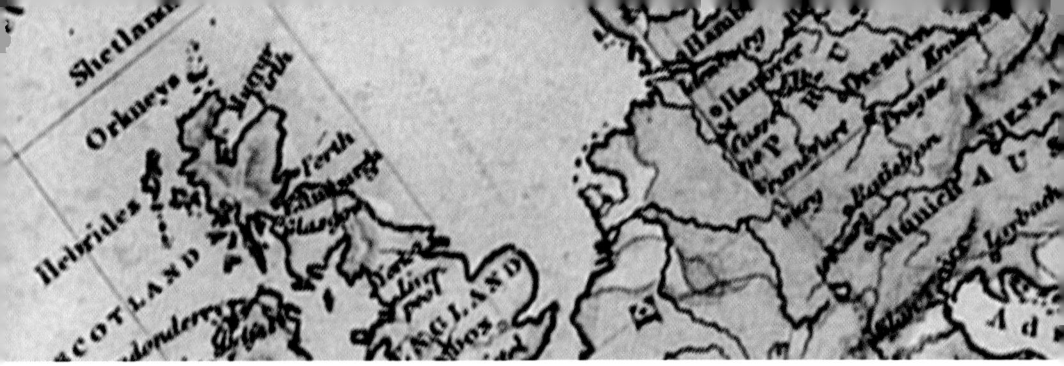
Orkneys
Hebrides
Forth

Common Core Aligned
READING QUESTIONS

1. **Why do the characters go on an eighty-day journey around the world? Find specific details in the text and art that support your answer.** *("Delineate and evaluate the argument and specific claims in a text, including the validity of the reasoning as well as the relevance and sufficiency of the evidence.")*

2. **List all the different methods of transportation that Jean and Phileas take on their journey. Next, write down a few advantages and disadvantages of each particular form of travel.** *("Read closely to determine what the text says explicitly and to make logical inferences from it; cite specific textual evidence when writing or speaking to support conclusions drawn from the text.")*

3. **Make a list of all the obstacles the characters in this book face on their journey. How do they overcome their obstacles?** *("Read and comprehend complex literary and informational texts independently and proficiently.")*

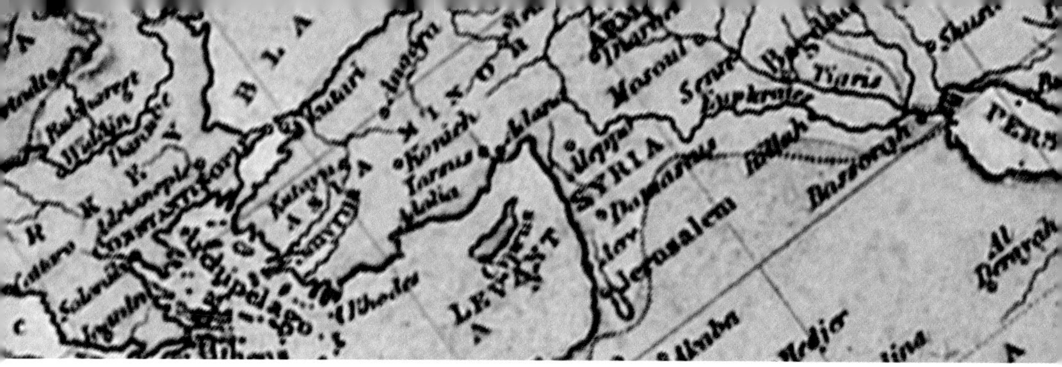
SYRIA
LEVANT
Jerusalem
Euphrates
Tigris

Common Core Aligned

WRITING QUESTIONS

1. **Draw a map that includes a destination the group travels to in this book. Then write a description of the location. What did the characters experience there?** *("Write informative/explanatory texts to examine and convey complex ideas and information clearly and accurately through the effective selection, organization, and analysis of content.")*

2. **Imagine you are one of the characters in this book. Write a postcard to a friend or a family member about your journey. What will you tell them about?** *("Produce clear and coherent writing in which the development, organization, and style are appropriate to task, purpose, and audience.")*

3. **Write four paragraphs about your favorite character. Why do you like that character the most? Identify areas in the text and illustrations that show why you like the character.** *("Write informative/explanatory texts to examine and convey complex ideas and information clearly and accurately through the effective selection, organization, and analysis of content.")*

READ THEM ALL!

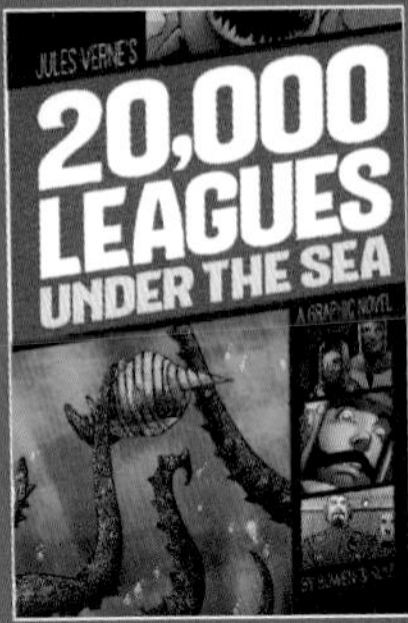
JULES VERNE'S
20,000 LEAGUES UNDER THE SEA
A GRAPHIC NOVEL

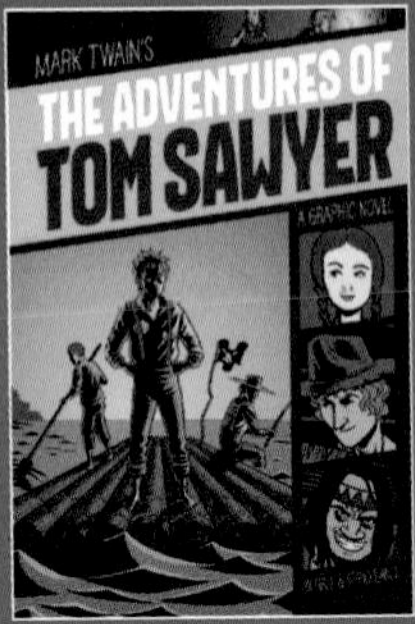
MARK TWAIN'S
THE ADVENTURES OF TOM SAWYER
A GRAPHIC NOVEL

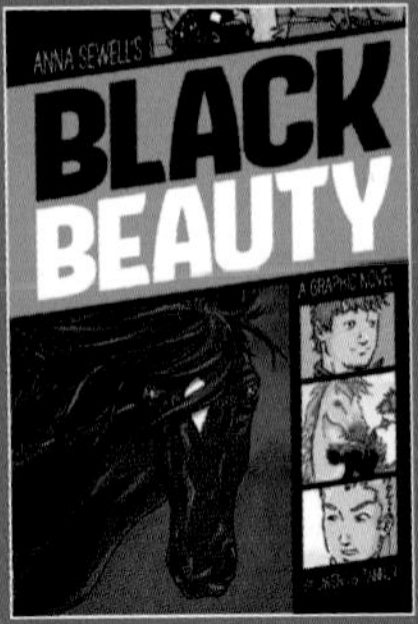
ANNA SEWELL'S
BLACK BEAUTY
A GRAPHIC NOVEL

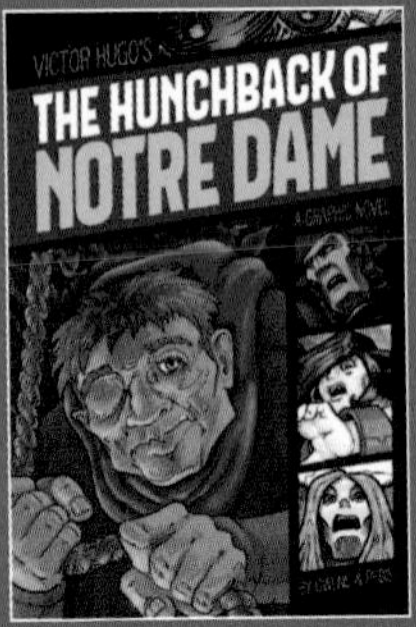
VICTOR HUGO'S
THE HUNCHBACK OF NOTRE DAME
A GRAPHIC NOVEL

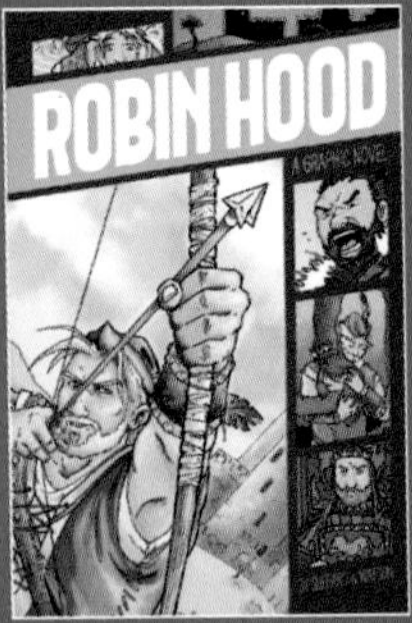
ROBIN HOOD
A GRAPHIC NOVEL

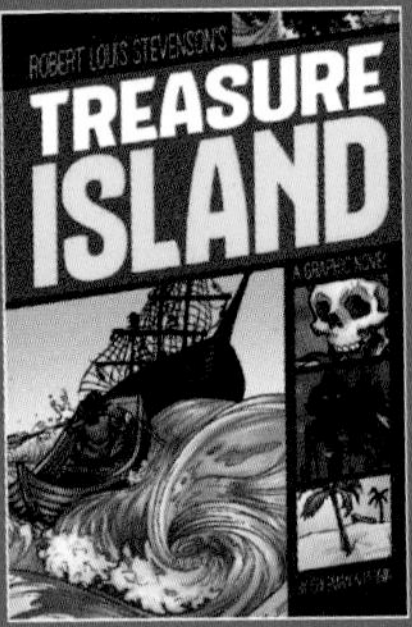
ROBERT LOUIS STEVENSON'S
TREASURE ISLAND
A GRAPHIC NOVEL

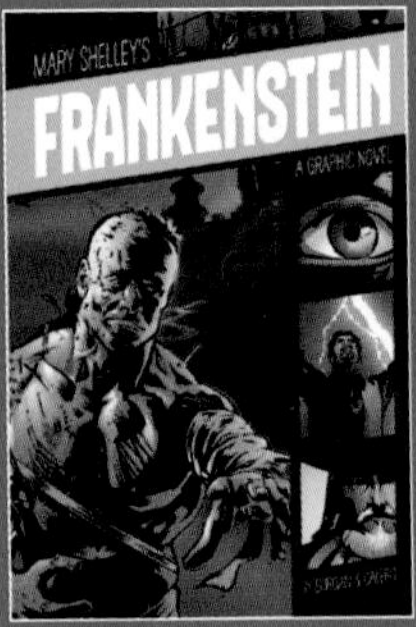
MARY SHELLEY'S
FRANKENSTEIN
A GRAPHIC NOVEL

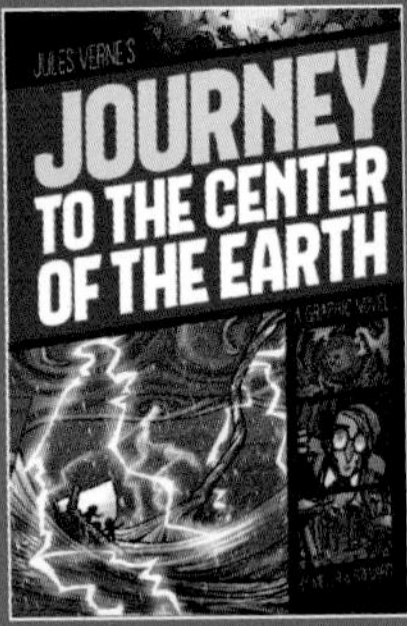
JULES VERNE'S
JOURNEY TO THE CENTER OF THE EARTH
A GRAPHIC NOVEL

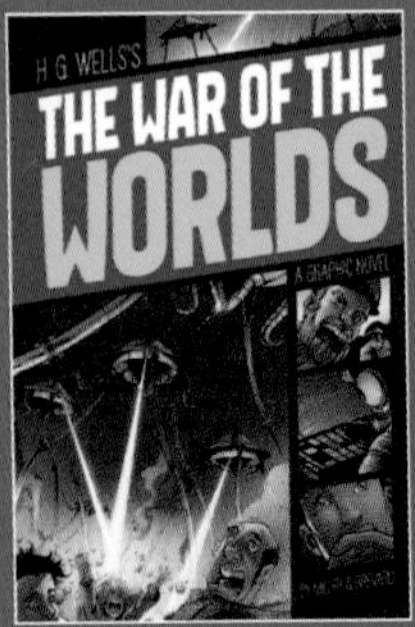
H. G. WELLS'S
THE WAR OF THE WORLDS
A GRAPHIC NOVEL

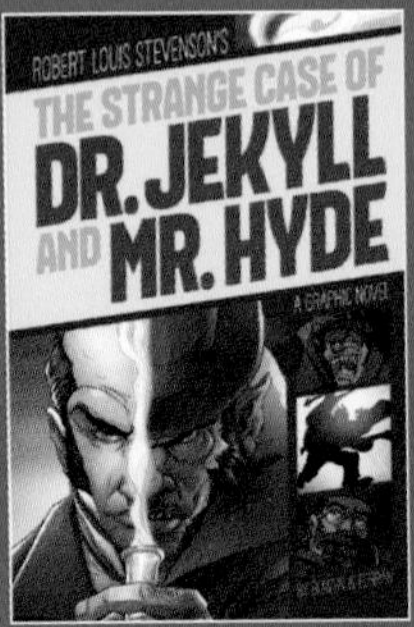
ROBERT LOUIS STEVENSON'S
THE STRANGE CASE OF DR. JEKYLL AND MR. HYDE
A GRAPHIC NOVEL

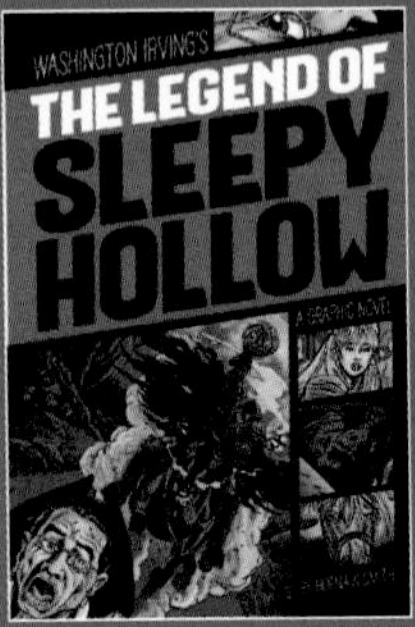
WASHINGTON IRVING'S
THE LEGEND OF SLEEPY HOLLOW
A GRAPHIC NOVEL

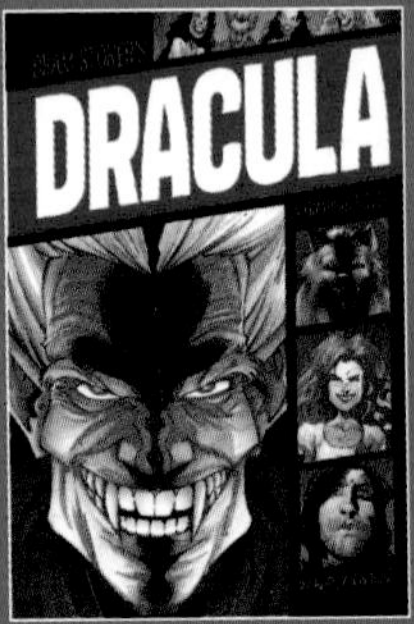
DRACULA

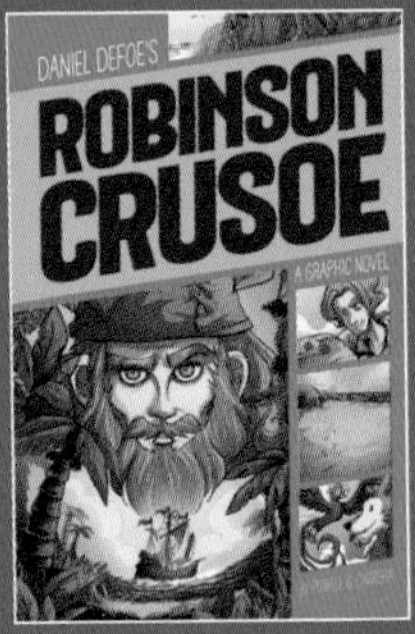
DANIEL DEFOE'S
ROBINSON CRUSOE
A GRAPHIC NOVEL

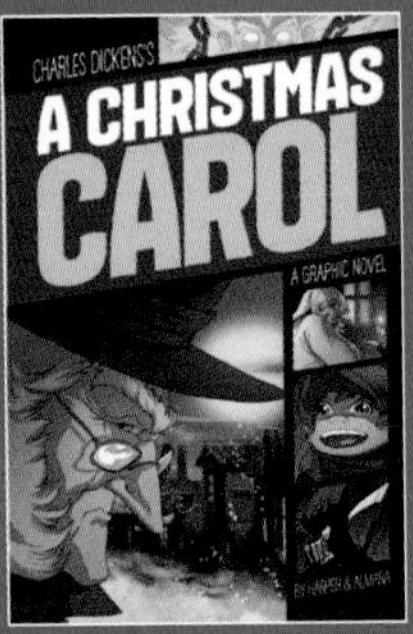
CHARLES DICKENS'S
A CHRISTMAS CAROL
A GRAPHIC NOVEL

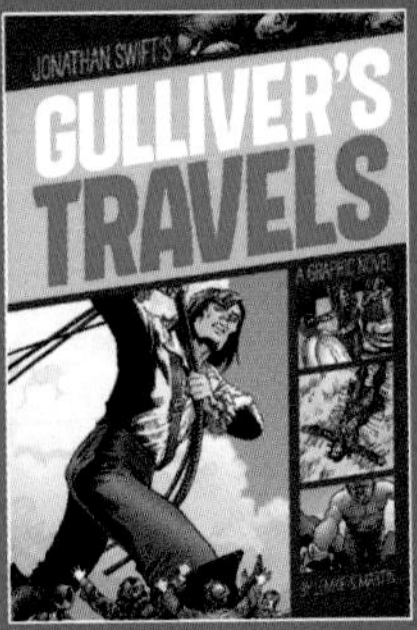
JONATHAN SWIFT'S
GULLIVER'S TRAVELS
A GRAPHIC NOVEL

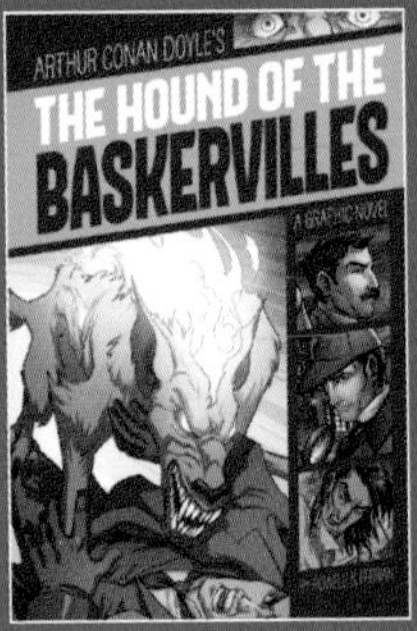
ARTHUR CONAN DOYLE'S
THE HOUND OF THE BASKERVILLES
A GRAPHIC NOVEL

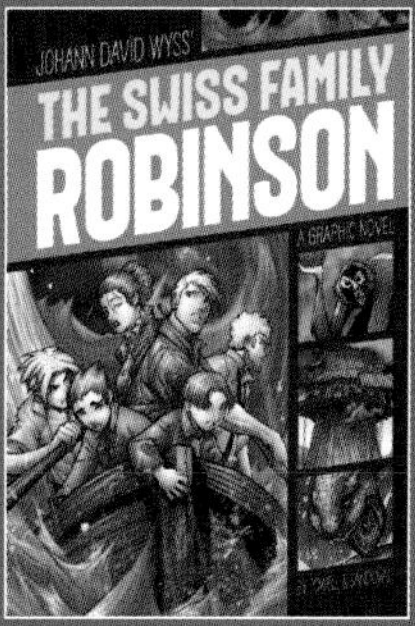
JOHANN DAVID WYSS'
THE SWISS FAMILY ROBINSON
A GRAPHIC NOVEL

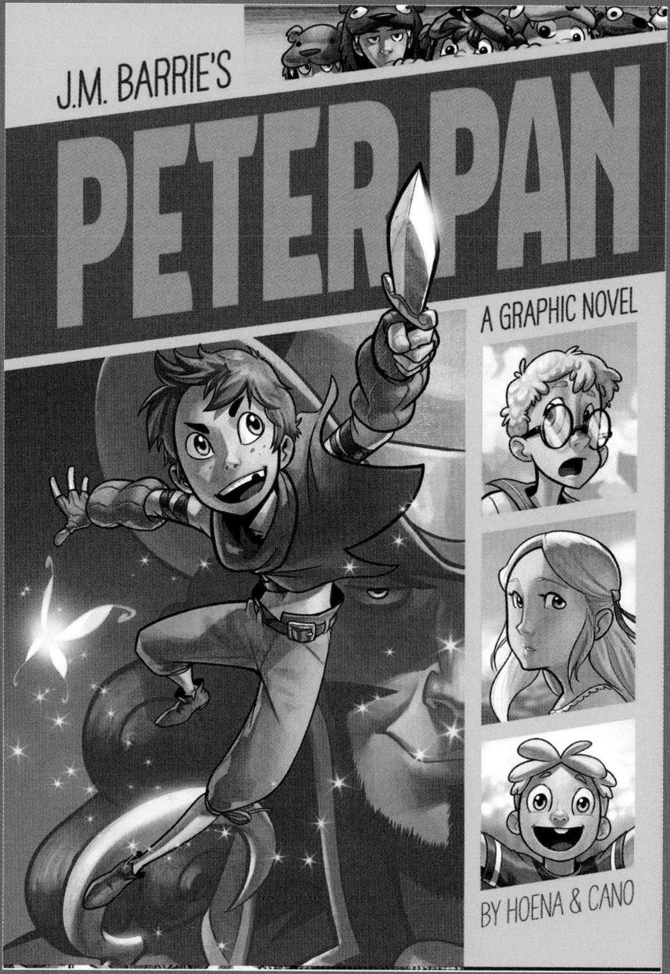
J.M. BARRIE'S
PETER PAN
A GRAPHIC NOVEL
BY HOENA & CANO

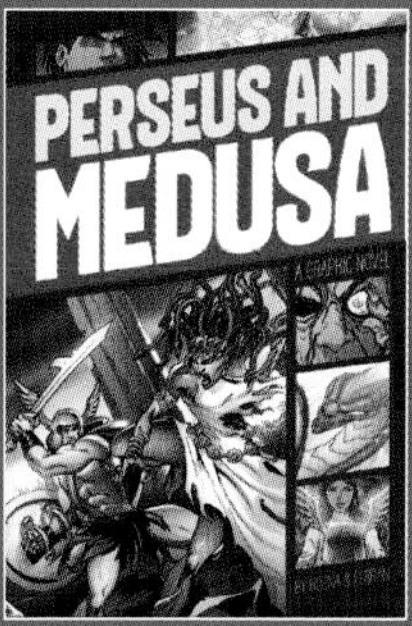
PERSEUS AND MEDUSA

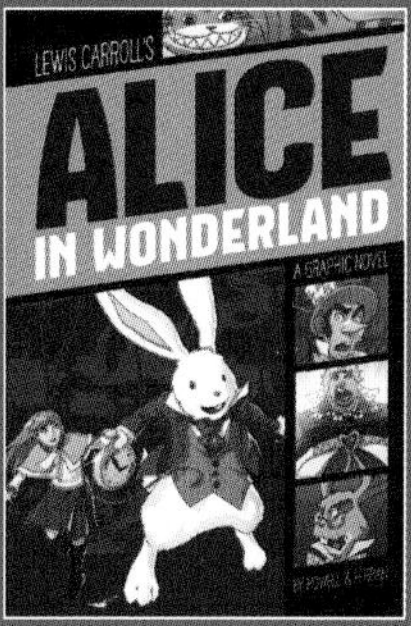
LEWIS CARROLL'S
ALICE IN WONDERLAND
A GRAPHIC NOVEL

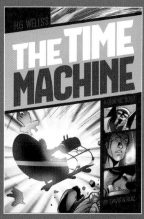

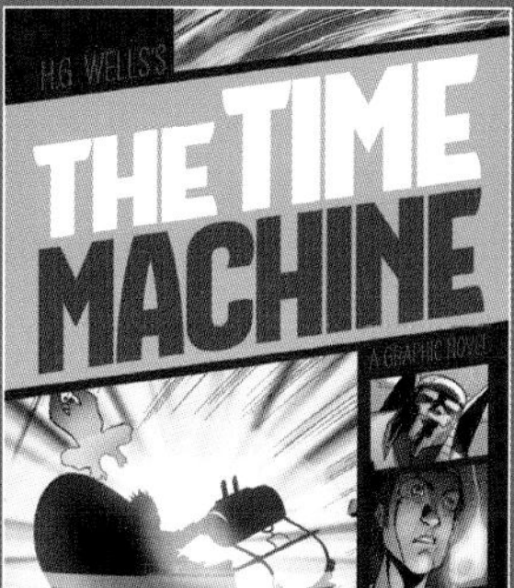
H.G. WELLS'S
THE TIME MACHINE
A GRAPHIC NOVEL
BY DAVIS & RUIZ

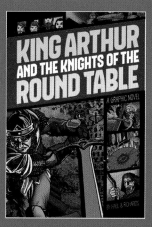

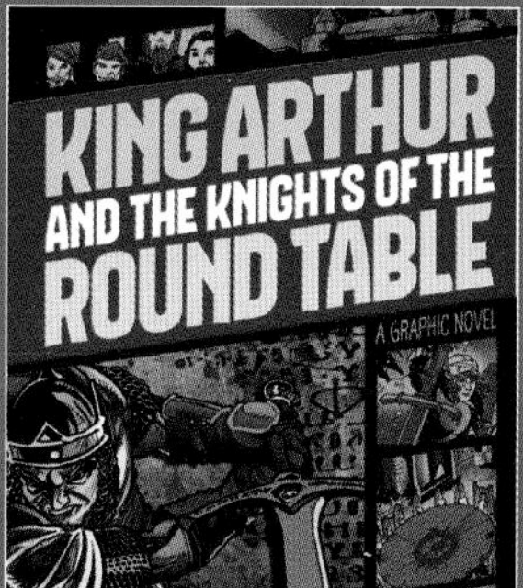
KING ARTHUR AND THE KNIGHTS OF THE ROUND TABLE
A GRAPHIC NOVEL
BY HALL & RICHARDS

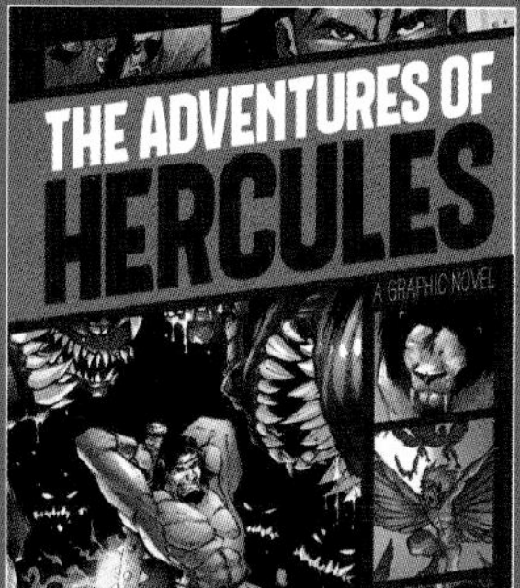
THE ADVENTURES OF HERCULES
A GRAPHIC NOVEL
BY POWELL & RUIZ

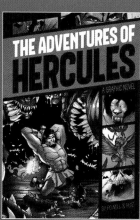